The Malignant Dead

C L Raven

Copyright © 2015 C L Raven

Cover by River Rose

Edited by Emma Adams

All characters in this book are completely fictitious. Any resemblance to any person living or dead is purely coincidental.

All rights reserved.

ISBN-10:- 1511431245
ISBN-13: 978-1511431248

Set in Garamond

Other books by C L Raven:

Novels

Soul Asylum

Short story collections

Romance Is Dead Trilogy:
Gunning Down Romance
Bad Romance
Romance is Dead

Disenchanted
Deadly Reflections
Romance is Dead trilogy

For Neen. Thanks for joining us in all our Edinburgh adventures, hunting for ghosts, embarrassing ourselves on YouTube and always ending up in Frankenstein's. In the name of research, of course.

Chapter 1

1645. The year Scotland died.

Glazed eyes of the dead watched the cloaked figure creep through Edinburgh's cobbled streets, his beaked mask casting monstrous shadows that slunk along the crumbling walls. People edged away, whispering 'Doctor Death'. Where he walked, Death followed.

Rotting bodies lay entangled in the alleys; the June sun and north wind conspiring to poison the air with the foul odour of decay. One body groaned as black rats investigated her. Although her flesh had decomposed, she was still alive.

Dirty white rags dangled from windows, like hanging men left on gallows for the city to witness their shame. Retching coughs and screams smothered the pitiful moans. Death no longer loitered in the shadows, veiled beyond people's nightmares; he prowled the streets, taking people where they stood. There was nowhere left for them to hide.

The figure stopped at a door. Red paint dripped like blood from a mortal wound.

May the Lord have mercy on our souls.

The words scrawled above the foot-long cross filled McCrae not with hope, but dread.

McCrae touched the cross. "There is no mercy here."

He wiped the paint on his leather cloak, leaving a scarlet smear. He must be mad. He wasn't a doctor. He was yet to cure an infected wound, yet he hoped to cure the plague. He could not even see out of the damn mask. He adjusted it then leaned down to tuck his leather breeches into his boots.

He beckoned a watchman, who crossed the narrow wynd and unlocked the door, his pipe clamped between his teeth. McCrae stepped inside the tenement. Gloom swallowed him, the smell of putrefaction lingering despite the herbs hanging in the window. Smoke infused the air from the brimstone burning by the hearth.

The stench of Hell.

Mrs Calhoun emerged from the bedroom, her haunted eyes revealing Death had visited her home. McCrae nodded and entered the small room. Rancid odours stirred his stomach. A man lay on the bed, blankets clutched in his decomposing fists. A shrivelled rabbit's foot dangled off a leather thong around his neck. His mouth hung open, as though Death came before he finished his scream. Pus from the burst bubo in his armpit trickled down his blackened, festering skin. Flies crawled over his face. The buzzing of their wings became the music to die to.

McCrae stared down at him, gripping his bag. His hooded cloak felt heavy on his shoulders.

"I had hoped you could help me."

McCrae unrolled the man's nightshirt sleeves then picked him up.

"Don't do this."

He turned. Mrs Calhoun blocked the doorway, fingering the heart pendant around her neck.

"I cannot leave him to rot. The infection could spread to you, if it is yet to take hold."

"Don't undertake this role. It is not worth it."

"The Guild of Surgeons and Barbers' apprentice fee is forty shillings. I cannot afford that on a market trader's wage. I will quit once I have cured this pest and settled my debt with my friend James."

"John did not see a penny of the wage the council promised. He 'did not live long enough to earn it'." She gestured towards her dead husband. "Do you know how long John was the plague doctor? A *week*. How long have you been the plague doctor?"

McCrae glanced at the man in his arms. "Doctor Petrie is my first patient."

Mrs Calhoun's eyes brimmed with pity. "How old are you?"

"Twenty six."

"Do you know what awaits you?"

"I have read about the treatments."

"You won't find the cure amongst the pages of a book. All John's superstitions – the chicken tail feathers, plague water and frogs' legs he gave his patients – could not save him. That lucky charm around his neck could not save him. *Nothing* could have saved him. Not even you. His parents died three days ago. He could not save them. Next week, the new plague doctor will put *you* on the cart while your betrothed weeps at your bedside. Tell me then it is worth the money."

Mrs Calhoun walked away as McCrae carried his predecessor to the door. He knocked. The watchman opened it and McCrae stepped into dying sunlight, where a cart waited. He laid John on the bodies then followed the cart. John's glassy gaze fixed on him, as though forewarning him of the horrors to come. McCrae looked away.

A carriage jolted past, heading for the Flodden Wall, burdened with a family and their belongings. The mother averted her eyes and hugged a bairn to her, as though the mere sight of McCrae would infect her.

"You cannot outrun Death."

The wheels of the next death cart rolling behind him drowned out the fleeing carriage.

A man staggered along Cowgate, weaving between the cattle before falling to his knees in the filth. He vomited; blood spattering his hands, the street, and the dead bairn he embraced.

McCrae's cloak creaked as he knelt and reached for the bairn.

"No!" The man scrambled away, cradling her to his chest. "Yer the devil!"

"I'm yer only hope."

McCrae eased the bairn from the man's arms and placed her on a barrow between two dead women. The wheels trundled forwards, the death bell tinkling, the bodies' limbs flopping with the cart's jerky movements.

"Bring out yer dead!" echoed through the street.

McCrae helped the man up. "Where do you live–?"

"William."

William shuffled along Cowgate, which ran parallel to the High Street, and turned right into Borthwick's Wynd. He stopped at a door bearing a scarlet cross. McCrae ushered William inside, motioning to a watchman down the street. He locked the door from outside. McCrae's eyes slowly adjusted to the dim room, lit only by the hearth.

"I'm McCrae." The large beak muffled his voice. Sweet herbs, dried flowers and bergamot oil masked some odours but nothing concealed death's putrid perfume.

"You cannot help us, yer no doctor. Go back to yer market stall where you belong."

"I'm the only one willing to help you."

"Until the council's money runs out. I want John."

"John is dead. I can fetch his corpse from the cart if you wish but he will be as helpful to you as my family's linen would be."

Laboured breathing rattled from the bed in the corner. An elderly couple slept in another bed.

"Why do they lock us in?"

"Because if they didn't, more folk would die."

McCrae moved to the writhing fire and laid a poker in the flames. William wheezed, his legs buckling. McCrae crouched, removing a lance and a rag from his pocket.

"I'm sorry, this will hurt."

He unbuttoned William's shirt and pierced the apple-sized bubo in his armpit. William hissed as blood and pus burst from his decaying flesh. McCrae dabbed the weeping wound with the rag, swallowing the vomit threatening to choke him. Would he get used to the sights, the smells of this wretched disease? Would he live to see it cured? Or would he become just another corpse rotting in the pit while the city died above him?

"Why has this happened? We stopped bathing because Pastor Matthews said the dirt would keep the pest away and that God would punish us for our pride."

McCrae examined William's blackened fingers and green nails. "God punishes murderers, not folk who bathe." He collected the poker.

William flexed his fingers. "What's happening to them?"

"Yer body is dying around you." McCrae wiped William's brow then slipped a stick into his mouth. "Bite." He thrust the glowing poker into the bubo, the rancid smell of burning flesh tainting the air. McCrae heaved, clenching his jaw to stop himself vomiting over his mask and his patient.

William screamed.

McCrae's medical books and cadavers had not prepared him for treating the living dead. Corpses didn't scream.

McCrae ran to the door, pounding on it like a still-warm body begging to be released from its grave. The watchman opened it. McCrae fell to his knees and tugged off his mask, vomiting into the dirt. He rested his hands on his thighs, gasping in the warm air. William's decay festered in his nostrils. He heaved and spat.

The watchman chuckled. "They don't smell like linen, do they laddie?"

McCrae wiped his mouth and shot him a contemptuous look. "They're infected – what's yer excuse?" He stood, pulling on his mask, and entered the tenement.

"Is anyone else infected?"

"My wife, Agnes." William coughed, blood streaking his chin.

McCrae patted his shoulder with his gloved hand and approached the bed. The rough breaths of the dying had silenced. A woman on the straw mattress cradled a five-year-old lad. At the foot of the bed, an eight-year-old lass lay curled up, clutching a doll.

McCrae brushed the lass's damp hair from her face. A small bubo lurked behind her ear.

She shrieked and wrenched back. "Mammy!"

"I'm a doctor," McCrae whispered.

She gripped her doll, crying as he lanced the swelling. He examined the lad. Red roses covered his pale, sweaty skin. He hugged his mother, his eyes wide.

"Are they–?"

McCrae nodded. Tears trickled from William's red eyes. McCrae checked Agnes's pulse then lowered his head. "I'm sorry."

"No!" William pushed McCrae aside and hugged his wife. "Agnes!"

McCrae grabbed the bed. His heart ached at the thought of losing Katrein this way. William collapsed, pulling Agnes into his lap. He sobbed, kissing her face.

"Bring out yer dead!"

"I'm sorry William. I must take her." McCrae prised Agnes from William's arms and carried her to the door. He knocked. The watchman opened it, covering his face.

McCrae whistled and the cart stopped. He laid Agnes in the back.

"You must be the new fella. You'll get a reputation for killing yer patients." The barrowman chuckled. Grey sprinkled his dark hair, like stray ashes had fallen from the sky from the remains of the witches Scotland had burned. Even with the black rag covering his mouth and nose, McCrae recognised Hamish Reid.

McCrae patted the grey pony, Bran, who shied away. "That's why they call me Doctor Death."

"McCrae?" Hamish peered through the beak's round glass eyeholes. "Samhain's not until October. There'll be no begging and celebration this year."

"There'll be plenty of spirits to welcome."

"You should see him without the costume," Hamish's twenty-year-old passenger whispered.

"How are you, Hamish?" McCrae asked.

"Better than my passengers. They're a wee bit quiet today." Hamish jerked his thumb towards his cart then elbowed the woman beside him. "Though Katrein's broth is trying to kill me."

"Every day it fails," she replied. Hamish laughed.

"Katrein!" McCrae circled Bran, who nipped at him.

"Are you trying to frighten yer patients into their graves, Alex?"

"Some say evil spirits caused this, and the mask frightens them away."

"You believe them? For shame. I thought you were a man of science, not superstition."

McCrae helped Katrein down. She wore her black nurse's habit, her soot-coloured hair escaping her cap.

"Why did you not tell me you had accepted?" she asked.

"You'd try to stop me."

"I don't want you to die. The thought of riding in Hamish's cart with you dead in the back terrifies me. But you'll be a wonderful doctor. Even if you look like a monster."

"Folk will never accept me as a doctor. The way they would not be happy if the flescher became king."

"You do not accept the role you were born into. Folk cannot understand that."

"At least they don't have to worry about you becoming king." Hamish laughed. "Yer manners and fists would see you on the gallows, not the throne."

McCrae smiled, though they could not see it. He stroked Katrein's hair. "Stop riding in Hamish's cart. The dead could be contagious. I don't know what causes the plague, how it spreads. I refuse to believe this is an act of God."

"Witchcraft," Hamish said.

"It's a disease, not a curse."

"Just because you cannot see the world beyond this one, does not mean it's not there. If they were not witches, why did the council burn them?"

"If this is caused by witchcraft, why did it not stop after Agnes Finnie was executed in March?"

"She's not the only witch in Edinburgh."

Katrein smiled at their exchange. "I'm treating a woman's broken ankle in Grassmarket. Hamish is taking me."

McCrae groaned. "Will you ever obey rules?"

She stood on her toes and kissed his mask's cheek. "If you wanted someone obedient, you would not be marrying *me*."

"Each one of my grey hairs is caused by trying to control this one," Hamish said.

Katrein hitched her skirt and climbed into the trap. "If my broth hasn't killed my cousin, the pest won't kill me."

Hamish leaned over and tugged McCrae's beak. "Yer not putting me in the back of my cart, birdman." He flicked the reins and Bran walked on. "Bring out yer dead!"

Katrein blew McCrae a kiss.

THE MALIGNANT DEAD

Searchers entered tenements, scouring for the dead, the dying and the diseased. One searcher emerged, her face grim as she painted a crimson cross on the door and hung a white rag from the window. McCrae sighed, each cross a stain on his soul. Paint dripped down the wood, bleeding into the words.

May the Lord have mercy on our souls.

Chapter 2

"Gardyloo!"

Windows opened and buckets of waste were emptied onto the street.

"Hold yer hand!"

McCrae ducked into a doorway as excrement splattered the cobbles. Rats squeaked and scuttled. He pulled his cloak tighter around him. A rat ran over his boot, its whiskers twitching before it wriggled beneath a pile of hay. When no more shouts came, McCrae squelched out of Borthwick's Wynd on to Cowgate. Cowgate had the misfortune of being at the bottom of the sloped city so was ankle-deep in waste. The only thing that smelled worse than the plague was Edinburgh itself.

McCrae turned left up Candlemaker Row. Wind was the only thing wandering the street. Even in the summer, it haunted the labyrinthine city, its mournful moans whispering through people's dreams. The stench of tallow was a permanent resident amongst the candle makers, who were placed here to keep the smell of tallow out of the burgh.

A lone lantern flickered in Gray-friar Kirkyard, casting shadows that danced to Death's heartbeat.

McCrae slunk through the black gates, greeting the gravedigger, Gregor, beside the full pit.

"Don't know what's worse," Gregor grumbled, pulling his cap over his white hair, "the digging or the stench."

"Be careful; you don't want to dig yer own grave. When the living are gone, who will bury the dead?"

"I buried my helper yesterday. The crows can have the corpses."

A crow cawed in the nearby tree, anticipating his feast. Bodies tumbled from a cart into their eternal resting place like the waste thrown from windows when the tenth hour of the night arrived.

"Only the rich get graves," Gregor said. "We cannot leave them rot on the streets while we bury others. The dead know no better."

"The living do."

"Then save them. Or by dawn there'll be another pit." Gregor shovelled earth over the entwined bodies. It rained against their marbled skin, seeping into their mouths and eyes. "Folk are dying faster than I can bury them."

"This seems…barbaric. I knew them." He pointed. "John Petrie, my predecessor. Gordon, the candle maker, Mrs Firth, who looks after orphans."

"Yer born, you live, you die, you rot. But with this cursed pest you rot before you die." Gregor scowled. "My wife is in this pit. Don't you think I would bury her properly if I could? When this pest is over, we'll have to remember the dead. There won't be a stone over the grave to help us."

McCrae turned to leave. Guttural groaning pricked his ears. He whirled around, raising his lantern. Eerie shadows danced over the corpses as though death spirits celebrated the end of days. "Are you sure they're all dead?"

"I'm not the doctor."

McCrae stepped forwards, the lantern swinging shadows over the earth-shrouded bodies. Silence swept through the kirkyard.

"First day nerves." McCrae laughed tentatively.

Gregor grunted and returned to his task.

McCrae left the kirkyard, slipping into the darkness while the city weakened and died.

***

A death cart passed below the Old Tolbooth Jail by St Giles Kirk on High Street. Fergusson's fists curled. The corpses seemed to glare at him accusingly. Herbs hanging in the windows banished death's fetid odour. He studied the Edinburgh Castle portrait adorning the wall. In the light, airy chamber with the polished marble floor and ceiling-high walnut bookcases, he could believe the plague was merely a ghost story bairns told each other in the dark.

"We must stop the carts coming this way. If I wanted to see corpses I would drive one of those wretched things myself." Fergusson joined his fellow councillors, Douglas and Kilbride, behind the walnut desk. "They must only be on the streets between nine p.m. and five a.m. That way, nobody shall suffer upon seeing them."

"This pest is spreading faster than we anticipated," Douglas said. Like the other councillors, he was in his mid-forties. He had a large build, sandy hair and bushy whiskers on his jowls. He read the accounting sheets before him. "We can barely afford to pay the living and we are running out of money to bury the dead."

"We could join the rest of the council in Stirling," Kilbride suggested. He was the shortest of the three, with a blossoming paunch and large moustache. "The young one, Alasdair Blair, left yesterday. We are the only ones left."

"We are not fleeing like rats," Fergusson retorted. "Do you wish to leave Edinburgh to the thieves, the vagabonds? Maybe the plague-riddled would like to manage the finances."

"The wealthy are leaving. Soon only the thieves, vagabonds and plague-riddled will remain."

THE MALIGNANT DEAD

Douglas sighed. "I propose we cease all trade to and from Edinburgh. We cannot risk people bringing disease with them, and we cannot risk it leaving Edinburgh. People are scared. They are attacking strangers, blaming them for spreading it. On Saturday, some unfortunate deformed man was accused of causing the pest and hanged outside the inn. There is talk of witchcraft."

Fergusson frowned. "We burnt all the witches."

"The infected are confined to their homes, except when bringing out their dead," Kilbride said. "What else can we do? Burn them in their homes?"

"It might come to that," Fergusson replied. He was the tallest and slimmest of the councillors, with short brown hair and a neat, wide moustache.

Douglas and Kilbride exchanged uneasy glances. Fergusson sighed. They lacked the courage to save the city.

Douglas covered his mouth. "That is barbaric. People would never forgive us."

"At least they would be alive to pass judgement. The dead are past the ability to forgive," Fergusson said. "Anyone caught fleeing Edinburgh will be fined. We must contain this. We could follow Leith's example and banish the diseased to the Burgh Muir ludges by the Chapel of St Roque."

"If the patron saint of the plague-stricken cannot help them, nobody can," Kilbride said. "Who should we send first?"

"We could start with the homeless. They are as bad as the rats. We shall give the barrowmen an extra shilling to take them. Anyone who lives with an infected person shall also be sent to the Muir. Once it is proved that they are not infected, they shall be allowed to return. We will need bailies to oversee the transportation and cleansing."

Douglas noted the decision in the ledger, the scratching of his nib the only sound in the office.

The tolling bell of a death cart passed outside the jail then faded. Fergusson's jaw clenched.

The door rumbled as if Death requested an audience.

"Enter," Fergusson said.

A man in a long leather overcoat, breeches, hooded cloak and beaked mask walked in, muddy footprints stalking him. Fergusson scowled. It was too late to request he remove his boots. Fergusson's heart thumped as the monstrosity fixed his glass eyes on them, his breathing raspy. Fergusson groped in the desk for a weapon. Maybe Douglas was right. Maybe the witches were not dead.

"Who the devil are you?" He hoped the stranger did not notice the tremor in his voice.

"McCrae." His voice was muffled.

"Who?"

"The new plague doctor."

"Take that God-awful mask off. It is not Samhain."

McCrae lowered his hood and unbuckled the mask. His dark hair was tousled, strands sticking to his forehead. Two days' stubble growth shadowed his jaw. He looked more like a ruffian than a doctor. Fergusson doubted the young man's claims of attending the Guild of Barbers and Surgeons. Were they really allowing his sort to join? They must be desperate for doctors.

McCrae removed his glove and spiked up his hair. "You said I would be paid once I started. Three days ago."

Fergusson clasped his hands in front of him. "You will be paid at the end of the week."

"Is there any chance I could…have some now? I heard tobacco cures the plague and I'd like to buy enough for everyone. It would be better to prevent it rather than trying to cure it. I don't know if it can…be cured. Folk don't know they are infected until they are sick."

Fergusson fixed him with a cold stare, enjoying watching the urchin squirm. "You come in here, demanding your wage, then confess you cannot do what we are paying you for? We are not paying you to dress up and perform magic tricks. Do you think your hideous costume will *scare* the plague out of Edinburgh?"

"Tobacco might stop people inhaling it. Maybe it's…Edinburgh is filthy, sir. The waste on the streets smells worse than the plague. Only the rich can afford to have their waste taken away."

"Are you suggesting it's the *people's* fault they are dying? Perhaps you would like to inform them of your opinion as you remove their bairns' corpses."

"You misunderstand me. Perhaps you can pay someone to take away everyone's waste. This pest has been killing folk since December. Yer methods don't work."

"If you cannot cure them, we will hire someone who *can*. You will not be paid after three days."

"Mrs Calhoun said you didn't pay her husband because he died too soon."

"Can you cure the plague or not, McCrae?"

McCrae's green eyes were unreadable. His mask hung by his leg. Fergusson tore his gaze away. That mask would haunt his dreams.

"Aye."

"Then cure it." Fergusson picked up his quill and returned his attention to his notes.

"I need tobacco. And herbs."

Douglas cleared his throat. "McCrae, you will be paid handsomely at the end of the week. Until then, our money is spent burying the dead. The plague will spread faster if we leave corpses to rot in the streets. Come and see us on Friday. Right now, we have urgent matters to discuss."

All three councillors stared at their paperwork, relieved when McCrae's footsteps trudged away.

"Who does he think he is, demanding money?" Fergusson said.

Kilbride shifted in his chair. "He was hardly demanding. We could pay him a few shillings."

"What if we had paid Petrie? We would be bankrupt and without a doctor. That money is no good burdening his pockets at the bottom of a pit."

"Why offer such a large amount?"

"You think someone would treat the pestilent out of *kindness*? Nobody wants to risk their life on the malignant dead."

Douglas rubbed his face. "McCrae said people are diseased without realising. Perhaps we should ban public gatherings."

"There is an execution scheduled for Friday," Fergusson said. "People need to see justice being served or Edinburgh will descend into a city of vice and debauchery."

"We could hold the execution in private," Kilbride suggested.

"We will be taking away the people's entertainment."

"Kilbride is right," Douglas said. "Extreme measures must be taken. If a temporary end to public executions helps, it is a step we must take. We banned gatherings following weddings and funerals in March, this is no different."

"Very well," Fergusson said. "From Friday, executions will be private."

Douglas nodded. "The city has seen enough death."

Chapter 3

Hamish whistled as he tipped his cart. Bodies tumbled into the pit, like rotten vegetables tossed from the market stalls. Gregor leaned on his spade, smoke from his long-stemmed pipe spiralling into the night.

"Pleasant night!" Hamish called.

"If you find the stench of corpses sweet," Gregor grouched.

"They smell better than the inn on a busy night. We're in the best business! We'll never lose our jobs. Plenty of customers and we're working in the fresh air. We could demand a higher wage from the council and they'd pay because no-one wants this task."

"Riding with the dead all night has eaten yer brain."

Hamish smiled beneath his rag. "I had an extra shilling today for ferrying the homeless to the Muir. Maybe I should catch this pest and live in the ludges. They don't smell like Edinburgh does. And folk get fed."

Hamish lifted the last body, lowered him into the pit, then patted Bran's nosebag. If McCrae's beak saved him, it could save Bran. He glanced back. A man stood on the edge of the pit. Putrid skin peeked out beneath his torn clothes. Buboes protruded behind his ears, weeping blood and pus beneath the rabbit foot around his neck. Mud clung to his hair and clothing. His bloodshot eyes watched

Hamish. His mouth opened, earth spilling onto his bare feet.

"You don't scare me, John," Hamish said. "I work for the council. They're the scariest beasts in Edinburgh."

"Who are you talking to?" Gregor asked.

Hamish tore his gaze from Petrie. "One of my passengers is thanking me for the ride."

Gregor turned away, muttering. "Eaten yer brain."

Hamish returned his gaze to Petrie. All that stood before him was the fresh pit. Hamish rubbed his face. He climbed into his trap and flicked the reins. Bran walked on, swishing his tail. The lantern and the bell swung with the cart's movements. Hamish glanced over his shoulder. The phantom watched him leave.

Hamish waved. "Edinburgh's become a city of the dead."

***

"You tell folk you see ghosts, they'll burn you for witchcraft." Katrein joined Hamish by the hearth.

He smiled, ruffling her hair. "I'll tell them you bewitched me into seeing ghosts then we'll burn together."

"I'll poison you first." She flicked his nose.

"You haven't succeeded yet, lass."

"When I was a bairn, Mam said 'you watch Hamish. He sees things that are not there. But keep yer mouth shut. Edinburgh burns folk like him'. I was tempted, to see if they would. Yer lucky I liked you."

"Yer mam is wise. Did she also say you would marry a man who dresses as a bird and scares folk out of their riches?"

She laughed. "Alex is a good man. Though it wasn't his kind heart that attracted me; it was his handsomeness. And a glimpse I caught of him without his shirt. It set my heart fluttering." She winked.

"Yer wicked. But I would not let you marry anyone who wasn't good."

"You could not stop me."

"That's the only reason the plague hasn't got you, lass. Yer too bloody stubborn to die."

Katrein laughed as she scooped broth from the pot in the hearth. She broke a stale bread roll in two, passing half to Hamish.

"Is it poisoned?" He sniffed the broth. "Will I fall off my chair, clutching my chest while you plot to spend my riches?"

"A lady never tells. I may have spared you today."

She smiled. Hamish was thirty five, burly, with stubbled cheeks. He refused to wear the fancy facial hair most men adorned, with their combed moustaches or bushy whiskers.

"Never trust a man if you cannot see his face," he'd said.

"You wear a rag over yers," she'd replied. He'd winked.

Katrein finished her broth and stood. "I must see a patient. No propping yer passengers up beside you."

"I like to give them a wee bit of fun before the pit. Some are better company than the living."

"No more talk of ghosts! Folk are scared enough."

"Of the pest or Doctor Death?"

He laughed as she threw bread at him. Katrein gathered her bag and left the tenement Hamish shared with two other barrowmen. She pulled her cloak around her, her lantern creating monsters that crept beside her as she walked down the steep slope of Old Fishmarket's Close towards Cowgate. The nauseating stench of the poultry and fish markets filled the night air.

"Bring out yer dead!"

Katrein shivered. She would never get used to hearing that chilling cry. Bells tinkled as death carts roamed the streets. Screams, sobs and rattling death coughs filled the silence. Soft clicking reached her ears, reminding her of tales about the death watch beetle. She picked her away across Cowgate, hitching her skirts to avoid the rats that darted from the darkness.

"Nasty night for a lass to be alone." A man slunk from the shadows to her right. Katrein stepped back, squishing rotting vegetables. "Where are you going?" He edged closer. She retreated, her back striking the wooden wall of a tenement. A dirty white rag hung limply beside her, the paint on the door dried and cracked. "Perhaps you would care for company."

She glared, her fear tinged with anger. How dare he intimidate her for walking down the street! "Get out of my way before I fix it so you'll never lie with a lass again."

"Yer a spirited one. I should tame you. Teach you to keep yer bonny mouth shut and learn respect."

"I should stitch yer filthy mouth shut. Teach you to be respectful."

He shoved her against the tenement and squeezed her throat. Katrein gasped and drove her knee into his loins. The attacker doubled over, his face screwed up. She swept around his crumpled body, gathered her skirts and ran, her heart pounding. Her lantern jigged, the candle flickering then dying, plunging her into darkness.

"Katrein!"

A candle lantern outside the flescher's silhouetted the creepy costume of her betrothed. He placed a small bairn into a cart. Her heart sank. She treated that lass last week. She ran over, hiding her quivering hands in her cloak. The hem of her skirt soaked up blood that stained the cobbles from the flescher's shop.

"Where are you going?" McCrae asked.

"Visiting a patient. Her wound is infected."

"Where's Hamish?"

"Finishing his supper before he brings the cart out."

"I don't like you walking the streets at night."

"You don't want me riding with Hamish but you don't want me walking either? How will I see my patients? Maybe I could learn to fly."

"A broomstick would suit you. With a wee black cat sitting behind you."

She tweaked his beak then stood on her toes and kissed an eyehole. "Will you visit my parents? Dad is feverish and Mam is weary from caring for him."

"I'll accompany you until Hamish arrives. The plague isn't the only dangerous thing in Edinburgh. Thieves and murderers walk these streets."

"I have never stolen anything nor killed a man. But I did just kick one in the loins for being rude."

His hands curled into fists. "Where is he? I'll cut out his tongue so he can never insult you again."

"Perhaps he has crawled home to tend to his pain and wounded pride. Yer Hippocratic oath prevents you from doing harm. I'm not bound by that oath, so if I see him, I'll harm him on yer behalf."

She stole another kiss then darted into a tenement opposite.

***

McCrae knocked on the door. Katrein's mother, Morag, opened it and yelped.

McCrae swiftly unbuckled his mask and removed his glove to spike up his hair. "I'm sorry to startle you, Morag. Katrein asked me to visit Angus."

"My husband needs a *real* doctor." She shoved the door.

McCrae stopped it with his hand. "If I leave, Katrein will throw me into the Nor' Loch. Then dive in to save me."

Morag hesitated then opened the door. McCrae entered the cramped house and edged past her into the bedroom, where Angus lay in bed. Sweat clung to his pale, blotched skin. McCrae checked his pulse and opened his nightshirt. Red roses decorated his chest. A small bubo nestled under his armpit. McCrae swore and pulled his mask and gloves on.

"Yer not wearing that!" Morag said. "You'll frighten him into his grave."

"He has the plague."

"No! He's just feverish." She scuttled over and held Angus's hand. "You cannot burst in here and say he has the pest! They'll lock us in to die! In a few days he will be well."

"In a few days, he will likely die."

"Get out!" She pushed him towards the door. "I want a real doctor, not a linen seller with grand ideas."

"You won't *get* a qualified doctor. Not now he has the plague."

"He's feverish."

"Let me help him." McCrae broke free and placed a poker in the fire then returned to the bed, pulling a pewter box of leeches from his bag. He crouched beside the bed, laying the leeches on Angus's chest. "I'm sorry Angus, this will hurt." He placed a stick in Angus's mouth.

Removing a lance from his pocket, he burst the bubo. He fetched the poker and burned the wounded skin. Angus bit the stick. It snapped. Morag sobbed and thumped McCrae's back. He held the poker in place until he was certain the bubo had gone.

He took the stick back. Blood stained the splintered edges. "I need to examine you, Morag."

"Stay away from me!"

"Either let me look at you or I'll fetch Katrein and we both know she'll be much stricter than me."

Glaring, Morag rolled up her sleeves. Faint roses marbled her skin.

McCrae closed his eyes, swore under his breath then opened his eyes. "I'm sorry. You are infected."

Morag collapsed on the bed. "No."

"Undress so I can check for buboes."

Numbly, she removed her dress, hugging it to her. She whimpered as McCrae lanced the bubo behind her ear and burned it with the poker. She flinched when he laid the leeches on her body. After he finished, she pulled on her dress, refusing to look him in the eye. He returned the fattened leeches to their box, sorrow seeping through his veins.

McCrae swallowed, his throat burning as he handed Morag a pouch of herbs and tobacco, telling himself to pretend they were merely patients. "Burn the herbs and smoke the tobacco. It will keep the smell away. I'll return in the morning."

He stepped outside and saw Katrein standing on the road. He signalled to a searcher. She ran over.

"They're infected." He handed her a clean white rag from his pocket.

"What are you doing?" Morag demanded, guarding the doorway.

The searcher crouched and painted a red cross on the door.

"Mam?" Katrein dropped her lantern, hitched up her habit and ran towards the tenement.

McCrae caught her. "You cannot go in. They're infected."

"Mam!" Katrein fought him off. "Unhand me!" McCrae pulled her back, lifting her. "Put me down or I'll make sure you never have bairns!" Her heels drummed his thighs.

"Katrein!" Morag shouted.

McCrae winced. "Go inside, Morag."

The searcher ushered Morag back in and hung the white rag from the window.

"No!" Katrein fought to escape McCrae's arms as he wrestled her into a hug. She pummelled his chest. "Alex, put me down!"

"I'm sorry." He stroked her hair.

"You must lock me in."

"No."

"I'm no different to anyone else whose family has the pest. You must lock me in!"

"The council can hang me for all I care. I won't lock you in."

McCrae nodded to a watchman, who approached the house and made the sign of the cross on his chest.

The watchman locked the door.

Chapter 4

The iron key clacked in the lock. The watchman stepped aside as the door creaked open. McCrae stepped inside. The dying fire danced feebly, orange tendrils snaking out to lick his cloak as he passed. The table was set for breakfast, the pottage cold, the bread hard. Shrivelled herbs hung in the window. McCrae's boots clumped on the floor as he entered the bedroom.

Two figures lay entwined in bed, their eyes open, flies crawling over their decomposing skin. When he visited this morning, they had been clinging to life.

McCrae lowered his head. A better doctor might have healed them. All he could do was give false promises and a death sentence. He had no right to bestow the title 'doctor' upon himself.

Morag's bones cracked as McCrae prised her from Angus's arms. He carried her to the door and stepped into the dark. Hamish bowed his head as McCrae laid Morag in the cart. Katrein watched from across the street. Wind tugged her nurse's habit, her lantern casting shadows on her tear-stained face. McCrae offered a tentative smile she could not see behind his mask then returned for Angus. He placed him beside Morag. Hamish flicked the reins, Bran plodding through the street.

McCrae stepped towards Katrein. She ran after Hamish. When he stopped the cart, she bounded onto it.

McCrae chased the cart. "Kat!"

"I won't have my parents tossed into a pit like the rubbish thrown in the Nor' Loch. They brought me into this world, I'll make sure they leave it with dignity."

"You cannot reason with her, Doctor Death." Hamish brushed Katrein's hair behind her ear. "All you can do is hand her the spade and watch her dig."

"Gregor won't allow it." McCrae rested his hand on Katrein's knee.

"Then I'll strike him on the head with his spade and when he wakes, it will be done."

"Yer giving me grey hairs." He jumped up, nudged her over and flopped onto the seat beside her.

"What are you doing?"

"I may talk the authorities into not charging us. You'll strike them on the head with a spade and end up in the Tolbooth." He removed his glove and took her hand. "Spades are for digging, not fighting. That's why you never see soldiers running onto the fields wielding farm tools."

"What about yer patients?"

"Two hours won't stop the plague. Yer more important to me." He lifted his mask and kissed her cheek.

"Yer too good for me, Alex."

"I'm atoning for sins."

Hamish clicked his tongue after the next body was placed in his cart and steered Bran towards Gray-friar. He turned left through the gate, where Gregor would not see them, hopped out and removed Angus and Morag from the cart. He helped Katrein down. McCrae jumped out, his cloak billowing. He set his lantern on the ground. Hamish climbed back onto the cart and headed for the pit. He returned with two spades.

"I'll keep him talking." He relinquished the spades then left.

Katrein started digging. "You could get into trouble with the council and yer master."

McCrae stamped on his spade, driving it into the mud. "What kind of husband will I make if I let you dig a grave by yerself, hiding in the town while the authorities drag you away?"

"They would have to gag me or I'd scream loud enough to awaken the dead. Then I could have an army of the undead to fight for me."

McCrae removed his mask and gloves. He ran his fingers through his unruly hair, peeling it from his forehead. "You read too many books. I cannot even begin to tell you how impossible an army of the undead is. They cannot fight when they are too busy stopping their organs falling out."

Katrein threw a spadeful of earth aside. "You won't think it's impossible when I'm roaming Cowgate with them stumbling after me, protecting me from the lowlifes and murderers that stalk Edinburgh's streets."

McCrae tossed a handful of mud at her. "They'll burn you for witchcraft if they hear you talk of raising the dead for nefarious purposes."

She threw mud back. He wriggled as it slipped down his neck and back.

"You think I would not raise them for good purposes?" A smile teased her lips.

"You don't commit acts of necromancy then enlist their help to run the market. It matters not if it's for good or evil – it's a pact with the devil and it will see you burned."

They dug in silence for several minutes.

A thoughtful look crossed Katrein's face. "When you cut folk open, do you see their souls?"

"The body is full of blood and guts. There is no room for the soul."

"Perhaps it left the body."

"Or I misidentified the appendix. Perhaps that is the soul. It has no other uses."

Katrein wiped her hand across her face, smearing mud over her forehead. "I didn't realise it would be this hard. I pity Gregor."

"He gets paid."

"Doing things for love is more rewarding."

"Are you done?" Hamish hissed, creeping around the corner.

"We're halfway done," McCrae replied.

"It's enough. My passengers are more talkative than that miserable fiend."

McCrae heaved more mud from the grave. "Yer cousin plans to raise an army of cadavers."

"Alex thinks it would be necromancy," Katrein said. "I think it's the best idea I have ever had."

"If anyone would do it, it would be you, cousin. But you'll have plenty of time to accuse each other of wicked acts when yer married. I'll see if I can convince Gregor to join me in a merry song." Hamish trotted away, singing. "Ring a ring of roses, a pocketful of posies, ashes, ashes, we all fall down!"

McCrae jumped out of the grave. In the lantern's light, the grave resembled a burning pit in Hell. McCrae put his mask on then laid Angus in the grave. He fetched Morag and placed her in Angus's arms. Katrein's jaw clenched, tears glittering in her eyes. The pain shadowing her face made McCrae's heart ache.

Katrein sprinkled earth into the grave. She stifled a sob. "Goodbye." She bowed her head, tears escaping. She wiped them, smudging more mud on her face.

McCrae pulled her to him, wishing he could squeeze the sorrow from her. "There is no shame in crying, Kat."

He raised his mask and kissed the top of her head while she wept.

"Crying will not bring them back to life." She pulled away, tears snaking clean tracks on her cheeks. "Thank you."

"God knows what would have happened had I allowed you and Hamish to do this alone. You probably *would* have raised the dead."

They filled in the grave.

"I'm sorry I could not save them."

"The plague cannot be cured, Alex."

"I refuse to believe that. I *will* cure it. I wish I knew how."

***

The cadaver's chest lay hollow like an open grave, his organs resting in jars on another table. McCrae sat on his bed in the gravedigger's loft, staring at the body on the table. The corpse's arms and legs had been amputated and lay beside him. The heart sat on scales. McCrae rested his forehead in his bloodied hands. The skin on his palms and fingers felt tight where the blood dried.

"Are you waiting for him to awaken?"

McCrae smiled at the young man who entered his room. His fair hair was neatly combed, his doublet and shirt spotless, despite the gruesome task they had performed.

"I cut out his heart, James. Even the blood-drinking undead would not wake from that."

"You should lock your door. What if I had been Paterson? Imagine what he would do to you if he caught you with a stolen cadaver."

"It's not stolen – you paid Gregor for it. The council allow the Craft one body a year for dissection. We are merely accepting their offer. If the Craft allowed us to practise on bodies, we would not be forced to buy them. How will we learn through books alone? A book didn't teach me what it was like to burst a bubo. A cadaver did. This man had the beginnings of the plague. If I learn what causes it, I can cure it."

James sat beside him.

"Are you sure you want to sit so close? No-one will even look at me lest I infect them with a stare."

"Until I see you wearing a hooded robe and carrying a scythe, I refuse to believe you are Death himself." James cocked his head. "Though your costume does have a hood and you carry a stick. Maybe you are the modern version."

McCrae smiled.

"How on earth did you think up such a monstrous costume?"

"Doctors in France wear them. They're not dying like Edinburgh's doctors."

"You're taking fashion advice from the *French*?" James laughed. "My, you *are* desperate. We do not imitate the French – we fight them."

"We leave fighting the French to you English folk. They can succeed in killing you where we failed."

James approached the table and peered into the cadaver's chest. "I heard you put Katrein's parents on the cart." He picked up a leg and examined the cut below the knee. "Clean cut."

"I wanted to be a surgeon to save people. All I'm doing is watching them die."

James returned to the bed and squeezed McCrae's shoulder. "Death comes for us all."

McCrae straightened and pointed at the corpse. "Do you know why he was executed?"

"I care not. He is providing us with a body to learn on. That absolves his sins for me."

"He was hanged for concealing his wife's infection. The plague is killing half the city and they're hanging the other half!" McCrae leapt up, his leather doublet hanging open. "I'm foolish thinking I can cure it."

James pulled McCrae towards him by his doublet then fastened it. "I would say this is God's doing, but we are men of science and know better. Perhaps you should see if the infected signed the Covenant. If they did not, this is God's work. But disease does not care for such matters. Rich or poor, good or wicked, we all die in the end." He fastened the last button and straightened the picadils. "You are missing a button."

"I hope it's not in the corpse."

"Come to my rooms. I wish to show you something."

McCrae winked. "I have seen it; I wasn't impressed. And besides, I'm betrothed."

James laughed and collected the jar of lungs and a small unburst bubo McCrae had cut off.

McCrae stepped to the bowl of water perched on a stool and scrubbed the blood from his hands. His white shirtsleeves were rolled up and speckled with blood.

McCrae dried his hands on a cloth, gathered his bag and followed James to his lodgings on Niddry Wynd. Tables burdened with an array of flasks, bottles and alembics filled with coloured liquids took up half the room.

James crossed to the table and placed the lungs and bubo down. "I have been working on something."

He poured liquid into a goblet. It bubbled; thick vapour rising from the goblet and spilling over the sides.

McCrae pointed to the goblet. "I thought that only happened when the substance was noxious?"

"Nonsense. It is perfectly safe. I believe this pestilence can be cured. Or at least prevented. I have drunk a small amount of this potion every day. I even rode on Hamish Reid's death cart and lived to tell the tale. You must drink it." He poured the green liquid into a phial then proffered it to McCrae.

McCrae sniffed it and recoiled. "That smells worse than the pits."

"Tastes like feet."

"Is this why you have fallen behind on yer studies? Yer master will flagellate you."

"He would not dare. You might enjoy spending your days with your hands inside a man's chest, I however, find it…disgusting. Apothecary is my calling, but until they teach that separately, I am stuck dissecting corpses with the rest of you butchers. Medicine is what will cure diseases, not chopping off limbs and burning people with pokers."

"What's in it? Frogs' legs and ground unicorn horns?"

James laughed. "Herbs you use in that hideous beak, plus other ingredients. That phial's yours."

"Will I sprout wings or horns? Yer last potion gave Edward uncontrollable hair growth. Katrein won't marry me if I become a beast."

"That was unfortunate. But our fellow students are the only ones willing to be my test subjects. I assure you, this potion is safe." James spread his arms. "I have been drinking it for a week and I am as handsome as ever."

"In the dark." McCrae pocketed the phial. "If I turn into a centaur, I'll hunt you through Edinburgh."

"One sip a day. I have not tested the effects of ingesting more."

"Knowing you, it would turn me into a lass."

"I hope not. You would be ugly."

McCrae laughed. "I would not!"

"Alex, why did you take this godforsaken role?"

"I am tired of practising on the dead. I want to cure the living. And the council offered a handsome wage."

"Death is a high price to pay."

"I don't have a rich father to pay for my education. I don't even *have* a father."

"You have mine. We have been friends for sixteen years, since you stopped the hangman's sons from drowning me in the Nor' Loch for some invented sin. I would request more money from my father. I will tell him I need it for books. Or to marry an ugly lass who was once a man."

"I owe you forty shillings; I won't owe you more." McCrae picked up a phial of yellow liquid. "How did you persuade yer father to act as my guardian and sign my entrance papers?"

"I threatened to abandon surgery and work on your linen stall. He could not bear the shame of his favourite son—"

"Yer not his favourite."

"—his favourite son working in the market."

McCrae glanced sideways at him and smiled. "My dad beat me when he learned you taught me Latin and French. He never forgave you for encouraging my 'fanciful ideas' of being a surgeon. McCraes have always sold linen."

"If we do what has always been done, nothing will change." James elbowed him. "If the wretched plague kills you, rest assured, I shall take good care of Katrein. You can bequeath her to me in your will as thanks."

McCrae laughed. "Good luck! Only the other night she kicked a man in the loins."

James frowned. "I hope that fate would not befall me. I am rather partial to my loins."

McCrae chuckled.

"Here." James fetched a candle and handed it to McCrae. "I cannot bear the stench of your tallow candle. You smell peculiar enough without burning pig fat accompanying you."

"I can only afford tallow."

"I presume the council have not paid you your handsome wage?"

McCrae glanced out the window. "They'll pay me 'once the plague is cured'. They offered me the possessions of those I fail to save."

"What if it cannot be cured?"

"Edinburgh will die."

Chapter 5

Smoke drifted through the open door and windows; a tarnished soul condemned to Purgatory. It was perfumed with the sweet, woody scent of the burning heather and straw used to fumigate the Reids' home. Two puncheons of water stood outside the tenement should it catch fire. Across the wynd, McCrae and Katrein watched the foule clengers, their black cloaks bearing the diagonal white cross of St Andrew. They placed clothes and bedding on a cart.

"Take them to the Muir," a clenger told the barrowman. "Blankets are burned in the doocote, clothes go into the cauldron to be cleansed. The overseer will inform you when you arrive."

The barrowman nodded and flicked his reins, his cart rolling on.

The clengers splashed limewash over the walls.

"It's like they never existed." Katrein wrapped her arms around herself. "Everything they owned, gone. Their home, where I grew up, is empty like a coffin awaiting its body. The tenement is a mausoleum."

McCrae hugged her. "When the plague is banished, do you wish to remain here after we're married?"

Katrein shook her head. "When I lie in yer arms on our wedding night, it won't be in the room where they died. It would be as though we were lying together on their grave."

McCrae stroked Katrein's hair. "It's too sorrowful for you to watch this."

"Hiding from my grief will not repair their mortal coils. The clengers are washing away my memories too. Soon I'll be as empty as that tenement. Maybe then it will stop hurting."

McCrae pulled her close, kissing her lips. He closed his eyes, his fingers tangling in her hair, his other hand encircling her waist. His tongue flicked along Katrein's upper lip and she moaned, pressing against him. Her hands slid down his back, squeezing his arse. He jumped. She laughed.

Hamish stopped his cart. "Ooh the wedding night rehearsal."

They pulled apart.

"I'm reminding him why he's marrying me," Katrein replied. "So his head isn't turned by bonny lasses he meets on his rounds."

"Pus and rotting skin is not attractive." McCrae flicked Katrein's nose. "You might have yer head turned by some handsome lad whose wounds you treat."

"If you weren't the most handsome man in Edinburgh, I would not be marrying you."

"I thought it was my lavish abode and rich ancestors that won yer heart. And being the right hand of the future king. James believes he will be crowned, though he has no royal blood and has never fought a battle for King Charles, as surgeons are excused from military duty."

"James thinks he will be crowned before me? I'll behead him for treason when I'm queen. You had my heart when I saw you without yer shirt after James tripped you into the mud on yer way to the deacon's house. I followed you, waited until you left then 'accidentally' bumped into you."

"Yer utterly shameless."

She laughed and climbed into Hamish's cart, the wind whipping her hair.

"What have I said about riding in his cart?"

"You said I looked like a queen in her golden carriage."

McCrae laughed. "I did not."

"That is what I heard."

"We'll meet later."

"I'll find you when I have finished seeing patients." She nudged Hamish. "Onward, man!"

Hamish saluted then nodded at McCrae. "Don't kill any more patients until I have visited Gray-friar or they will sit between us as we ride through the streets, terrifying people with our gruesome cart of death!"

Hamish's cart trundled on, the bell jangling.

"You will both be the death of me!"

McCrae glanced at the Reids' tenement. Folk darted in, stealing whatever the foule clengers left behind.

McCrae headed for his room in the gravedigger's loft on Candlemaker Row and trudged up the stairs. The scarlet cross on the door had faded since it was painted in April. The room contained a bed, two tables, a chest for his clothes and a stand for the washbasin. A small window barely allowed light. Plaid linen piled up in one corner. He had not sold any since wearing plaid was forbidden, as it could conceal signs of infection. He could not bring Katrein here to live with him. There was more space in a pauper's grave.

Two months ago he shared the loft with a fellow student, George, until George found a new home in Gray-friar. Gray-friar was attracting more residents than Edinburgh's tenements.

The plague costume lay on the bed, like some nightmare creature had been slaughtered and its body tossed aside. McCrae was glad he was the one wearing it.

The dusty floorboards creaked as McCrae approached the bed. He dressed in the costume and tucked the breeches into the boots so disease would not find its way inside. He placed fresh herbs in the mask then put it on, lifting the cloak's hood over it, before slipping on the gloves. He opened the door, preparing for another battle with Death.

***

The only people haunting the streets were watchmen and barrowmen. McCrae pushed open the rickety door to the White Hart Inn, Edinburgh's oldest public house, which stood a few hundred feet from Grassmarket's execution site. The execution stage lay empty, awaiting someone's final performance.

Tobacco, ale and stale sweat suffocated the air. Straw crunched under McCrae's feet; stained red from previous brawls. A rotten tooth lurked beneath the strands. McCrae imagined the plague festering amongst the stalks. He ordered ale, dropping pennies into the bowl of vinegar on the counter. The barman pushed his tankard towards him then withdrew his hand.

Usually the inn was full of raucous men and cackling ladies of the night. Tonight, it was nearly empty. Nobody met his eye. The mood felt like a wake, except they weren't sitting up at night with a corpse, but a dying city.

McCrae nodded to a doctor then sat alone in the furthest corner. Folk averted their gazes. Even the hangman, Ketch, had company.

McCrae tossed the mask onto the table. "This role is cursed." The eyes stared at him. He swigged his ale and pushed the mask to face the other way. He put five people on the cart tonight. What would happen when the plague ran out of folk to kill?

"Want company?" A woman flopped onto the bench beside him. Her breasts protruded from her corset like two plucked chickens. She smiled, revealing crooked teeth, which reminded McCrae of crumbling gravestones in the kirkyard. Some were missing. Her breath smelled of rotting food. Her hand glided up his thigh.

McCrae grabbed her wrist. "No. I'm betrothed."

The prostitute froze, her gaze locked on the mask.

"Doctor Death!" She fled, tripping over her skirts.

McCrae finished his drink and grabbed his mask. People retreated as he stepped outside.

"Doctor!" A man ran over and grabbed McCrae's cloak. "My wife, Margret is sick. She's pregnant!"

McCrae donned his mask, his swinging lantern flinging shadows up the tenement walls. He stalked the man up Mary King's Close's narrow sloped wynd, his lantern casting the only light where even moonlight feared to enter. Laundry hung above him like defeated ghosts. The uppermost windows were devoid of rags. The rich had occupied the top floors before they fled the city.

The man climbed the tenement steps to the second floor and shoved the door open. Two women and two bairns were crammed into a small room. Ashes from a dying fire spiralled through the air, sprinkling the bare floor.

The bairns screamed and pointed. "Doctor Death!"

The younger woman hugged them.

McCrae warmed a poker in the fire's embers. "Who is free of infection?"

"Me, my mam, my nieces and Jim." The woman nodded at the man who had fetched him. "Please, help my bairns and my sister, Margret."

McCrae found no buboes on the bairns' cold, clammy skin. He fished the leeches out of their box, placing them on the bairns' trembling bodies.

"Do you have plague water?" their mother asked.

"It won't do any good."

"There is a man selling cures in the market."

"He's a quack. Don't buy anything from him."

"Mrs Jones said chickens' tail feathers will cure it."

"Chickens cannot cure the plague." He handed her a pouch of tobacco. "Smoke that. The bairns too. Burn these," he passed her some herbs, "and brimstone to banish the stench."

Jim ushered McCrae into a room with three beds. A woman shivered under holed blankets, cradling her pregnant belly. Tears streaked her grimy face.

"Save my baby." She clutched the horseshoe charm around her neck. Two lasses, aged two and four, slept at the foot of the bed.

"I can only help with the plague."

"Yer a doctor!"

"Not yet. If I try to deliver yer baby, I will likely remove a kidney."

McCrae fetched a wet cloth and wiped Margret's face. Strands of hair stuck to her forehead. She whimpered, her eyes closing as he parted her clothing. Red roses blossomed on her arm, a swelling nudging her groin.

"This won't hurt for long."

He lanced the bubo in Margret's groin. She yelped. He gave her herbs and bergamot oil then fetched the poker. Margret screamed. McCrae longed for the day when their screams no longer haunted his dreams. But he knew it would come when his humanity died.

McCrae took Jim aside. "I'll return in the morning. Hang a white rag out yer window."

"They'll lock us in to die!"

"If you don't, they'll *hang* you. You cannot help Margret if yer swinging from the gallows."

"How...long does she have?"

"If it takes hold...four days."

"Have folk survived?"

False hope was as helpful as frogs' legs. "Aye. But prepare for the worst."

McCrae stopped to collect the fattened leeches from the bairns. As he descended the steps to the street, the window scraped open. Jim pushed white cloth through the gap. A searcher approached the tenement armed with red paint. McCrae ran through the streets, slipping in the waste. He slid onto Grassmarket and burst through the inn's door.

He pushed a drunk aside. "Doctor!" He wrestled the mask off. "My patient has the plague. She's pregnant."

"There's nothing I can do." Doctor Sampson downed his scotch.

"Can you not cut the baby out?"

"Not without killing them both."

"You could *save* the baby! Without new life, Edinburgh will become a ghost town!"

"The bairn won't live to see sunrise."

"Yer supposed to save the lives of others. Not yer own. You don't deserve the title 'doctor'."

Sampson slammed his tankard down. "Do you wish for me to inform Paterson you were drinking in here tonight? I imagine that will earn you a beating."

"He can beat me until I can no longer walk, as long as you save Margret's baby."

"Laymen are hired in your role because doctors know it cannot be cured. You're barely old enough to shave yet you think you can play dress up and be a hero. Go back to your market stall, laddie. Sell your linen so families can bury their dead with dignity. Do not risk your life for the pestilent. They won't live long enough to thank you, and in the end, you will lie among their rotting bodies in the pit."

McCrae strode out, the door banging behind him. He pulled his mask on and sidestepped rats and the waste flowing down the sloped cobbled street. A pony trotted past him, its cart full of bodies, the driver dead at the reins.

McCrae ran after the pony and caught the reins. The pony flung her head up, her ears flattened. McCrae moved the driver into the back of the cart then hopped into the driver's seat. The pony wandered to snatch at a pile of hay on the ground. McCrae tugged the reins.

"Forward!" The pony scratched her face on her leg. McCrae flicked the reins. "Forward!" The pony snorted. "Hamish makes this look easy." He flicked the reins again.

The pony trudged on, turning left when McCrae tried steering her right. A rag fluttered in the breeze and the pony darted sideways, nearly tipping the cart. Eventually Gray-friar's gates greeted them. Hamish's cart waited outside.

Hamish laughed. "Are you a barrowman now?"

McCrae jumped out of the cart. "Do ponies do as they're told?" He looked pointedly at Katrein sitting in Hamish's cart.

She laughed and climbed out. "At least I don't eat yer coat."

He glanced down and chuckled, gently pushing the pony's nose away. Hamish led the pony into the kirkyard.

McCrae removed his mask.

Katrein shrieked then laughed. "I'm jesting." She spiked his hair up. "Yer face isn't quite as scary as that mask."

McCrae smiled, the nerves in his head tingling as her fingers scruffed his hair. "I was treating a pregnant woman on Mary King's Close. The infection's just starting but it's unlikely she or her baby will survive."

"I'll visit her; see if I can save her baby. Sadly, it would not be the first time I have cut a baby from its dying mother's belly."

"I don't want you catching the plague."

"My guardian angel says I'm too bloody stubborn to die." She pointed to Hamish, who emptied McCrae's cart. Hamish jumped back, swearing when a woman landed on his foot. "Though I doubt most folk's guardian angels drive death carts."

"First time I have heard Hamish called an angel."

"He hides his wings."

Hamish gesticulated to nobody. He walked towards them then stopped. He stepped sideways and scuttled to his cart.

"Leave me alone!"

McCrae raised his eyebrows. "Who is he talking to?"

"Ghosts."

McCrae snorted. "He's spent too long in the inn. Or he's been sampling James's potions."

"They're real, Alex."

"Perhaps he has an illness of the mind."

"He's not a lunatic! Just because we cannot see them, does not mean they're not there."

"If the ghosts of the victims are rising then Edinburgh really is the city of the dead."

***

The bell tolled, warning others what was coming. Hamish stared at the St Andrew's cross burdening the bailie's back as he walked before the cart, ringing his bell. The bailie's long stick prevented him from touching anything infected.

"I finally get to see the ludges folk talk about," Katrein said.

"Have you told the birdman yer coming here?"

"No. He would stop me. I'm no different to anyone else whose family had the pest."

The bailie stopped as they reached the Burgh Muir. Clengers used their hooked sticks to put clothing and belongings into the cauldrons to rid them of infection. Some were thrown into the dovecote to be burned.

An overseer approached the cart. "Name?"

"Katrein Reid. My parents died of the plague."

"Are you showing any signs of infection?"

"No."

"You are to remain here for two weeks and receive no visitors unless they are in the company of a bailie. Report to the quartermaster at the far ludge. If, after two weeks you are still free of infection, you will be allowed to return home."

The bailie walked on, Bran following. Two men hung from a gallows.

"What did they do?" Katrein asked the bailie.

"They stole infected clothing."

They stopped at the furthest ludge.

"You'll be safe here, Kat." Hamish hugged her. "Folk out here are surviving. And I will come see you when I bring others out here."

She kissed his cheek. "Bye Hamish. Be good." She hopped out of the cart.

"Come back to me. An Edinburgh without you is not one I ever wish to know."

Chapter 6

Fergusson stepped back as a ruffian marched towards him. His dark hair stuck out like a wild bush. Blood clung to his fingernails and stained his rolled-up shirtsleeves. His breeches hung over his scuffed boots, brushing the dirty ground. Dark stubble shadowed his cheeks – completely out of step with the fashion of pointy beards and wide moustaches. He was either a flescher or a murderer. Maybe both. Fergusson reached into his pocket, clutching his purse.

"Could I collect my wage before I treat my patients tonight?"

"Oh. It is you." McCrae almost looked human without that ridiculous costume. Though dressed in his everyday attire, his lack of breeding showed. "You dare to accost me in the street, asking for your wage? Did no-one teach you manners? Who is your master-surgeon? I should speak with him."

"Paterson. My patients are dying. They care more for their lives than they do for my manners."

"When it comes to the matter of wages, you will visit the Tolbooth and address the councillors properly. Not corner them in the market and ask for money like a beggar. I must take my leave; I have a hanging to oversee."

He moved to pass McCrae, doing his best not to touch him. As someone who was in constant contact with the plague, McCrae could be spreading it to his patients before the symptoms developed.

"It must be nice overseeing the hangings of folk whose only crime is being afraid of their fate if they reveal their relative is infected. Is that not murder?"

Fergusson turned around. "I beg your pardon?"

McCrae shrugged; a gesture that looked mocking and rude.

"Not revealing the infection is a crime for a good reason. If the infected are allowed to wander around, they could spread the plague to the entire city. We do not lock them in out of cruelty, McCrae, but out of necessity for the safety of the healthy. And if hanging them is the only way to make them obey, then I shall take them to the Tolbooth roof and watch them dance."

"We will see how strong yer belief in the crime is when it's *yer* loved one coughing up their lungs."

A short, squat man with small eyes and a large, squashed nose approached. "Is everything all right, sir?"

Fergusson's eyes blazed. "Everything is fine."

Andrews walked away. Fergusson sighed with relief. He could not risk being seen talking to such a scoundrel.

Fergusson locked eyes with McCrae. "You will speak to me in the council offices or not at all."

"I have been to the offices. Twice. You didn't pay me."

"You understood the terms when you accepted the position."

"I didn't think it would take this long."

Neither did Fergusson. Petrie died swiftly. "You will treat me with respect or I will make sure you never become a doctor in Scotland. You can spend your days penniless on the market stalls like your father and his father before him. I imagine your linen would sell well right now – people could shroud their dead in it."

McCrae fixed him with a cold stare. "You have to *earn* respect. Sir."

Fergusson clenched his fists. No. He would not stoop to this man's level by brawling in the street like the peasants in Grassmarket once the inn closed its doors.

Fergusson marched away. He would find someone willing to treat the plague-riddled then he would fire McCrae. Maybe have him removed from Edinburgh. If that wretch thought he was getting paid this week, he could think again. There were many ways to teach a man respect. McCrae would soon learn of them.

***

"I thought he would punch your nose through your face." James slung his arm around McCrae. "That will ruin your good looks. It is unwise to anger the council."

"When have you known me to behave wisely?" McCrae glared after Fergusson. He wished Fergusson *had* punched him. Nothing would give him greater pleasure than knocking him into the filth.

"Do you see that man Fergusson is talking to?"

McCrae craned his neck to see a man wearing a cap. "That's not a man, that's a troll."

"His name is Andrews. Fergusson's lackey. He will do any task for a coin, no matter how sinister."

"Trolls are not known for their good natures."

"A few years back, an innkeeper attempted to blackmail Fergusson. The man was found floating in the Nor' Loch. Andrews was the last person seen with him."

"You think Andrews will throw me in the Nor' Loch for requesting the wage they promised?"

"For disrespecting Fergusson."

"Respect must be earned. It's not handed down with inheritance."

"He is wealthy; he is allowed to treat you like filth. You are poor, therefore scum in his eyes. And you smell odd." James sniffed him.

"If Andrews throws me in the loch, I'll drag him down with me. I won't die a witch's death at the hands of the councillor's pet."

"My father said your biggest problem was not your lack of money, it was your mouth. There are ways to speak to those of more power and wealth. Arguing in the street is not one of them."

"I was denied the privilege of conversing with the wealthy."

"Nonsense!" James playfully punched McCrae's arm. "You converse with me all the time."

"Yer different."

"Did you learn nothing from the beating Paterson gave you for your insolence? I believe I perfected my skill whilst treating your wounds." James's fingers danced down McCrae's back as they walked through the market.

McCrae's back tingled at the memory. "Rich man or poor man, if he's being rude, I will punch him to the floor."

James tutted. "Not when he pays your wages."

"I'll visit him later in his offices, in my costume. It offends him."

"That is your idea for getting your wage? Frighten it out of them?"

"It works on Samhain." He laughed.

"If you do not hold your tongue, the councillors will stick your head on the highest spike of the Tolbooth's northern gable before you are paid."

"I'll have a lovely view of High Street."

"I shall wave to you from the castle when I am crowned king."

"You've been drinking too many potions."

"James is a king's name. There have been six kings of Scots with my name. Only three have had yours."

"It's a cursed name. Several King Jameses died foolish deaths."

"That fate shall not befall me."

"Besides, the king stays in London. Where you should be."

"What use am I in London? Here I can follow Andrews, make sure his intentions towards you are honourable."

"He won't ask for my hand in marriage."

"I should hope not! I believe you promised *me* your hand."

"Did you have a sword to my throat?" McCrae smiled. "Andrews will see yer fine clothes before you see him." He tugged James's doublet.

"I shall dress like a ruffian. Lend me some clothes."

McCrae laughed and swatted James's arm. "Cankerblossom."

James roared with laughter. "Is there a reason for your cheerful temper?"

"Katrein asked Hamish to take her to the ludges on Burgh Muir. She must stay there for two weeks."

"Perhaps it will be for the best. Many folk have returned from the Muir perfectly healthy."

Traders who had known McCrae since birth lowered their gazes when he approached.

"They think I am selling my soul," McCrae said.

"It matters not what they think. They will soon change their minds when they need you."

The flescher held out beef on a hook while his customer picked it off then dropped her coin into a plague stone. The stone stood at three feet high, on the edge of the market. The top was filled with vinegar. Even money could carry the plague. Normally the market would be busy; traders shouting their wares, customers talking as they crowded around the stalls. Now they traipsed to the plague stone in silence, their neighbours too sick, too dead or too scared to venture outside.

"Why do you stay, James? Wealthy folk have left. Paterson said they may bring graduation forwards so the students can leave too."

"Where would I go? There is plague beyond these walls."

"Stirling? Glasgow?"

James laughed. "*Glasgow*? You have been inhaling too many herbs. People are sent to Glasgow, they do not go there."

"Join yer father at Bethlehem hospital in London."

"I do not run from a fight, Alex. That is why Ketch's boys nearly threw me in the loch. Without me, who would stop you from tossing the councillors into the loch? Katrein would grab their feet and help you."

They walked past empty stalls that had thrived last year.

James stopped at a stall and picked up a phial of powder. "What is this?"

"Powdered unicorn horn," the trader replied. "It cures the plague. Please don't touch anything."

James sniffed the powder then tipped some onto his fingertip and tasted it. "How odd, it tastes like dirt and flour. What part of Scotland did this unicorn come from? I have never seen such a beast walking down Grassmarket. Alex, have you seen any unicorns?"

"No. Perhaps they have all been turned into plague cures."

James picked up a jar of frogs' legs. "I never knew frogs had curing properties." He plucked up some feathers. "*Chickens* can cure the plague? Here we are, eating them and wasting their feathers for pillows. Alex, you should consider hiring a chicken as your nurse." He put the phials down then darted across to another stall and snatched a black hen from the ground. He carried the protesting bird back to McCrae. "Your new nurse. You do not need me anymore."

"As long as she isn't as strict as you, I'll take her."

The owner glared. "If yer not buying anything, leave my stall."

James rolled his eyes and set the hen free. She puffed up her feathers and shook them, before running away.

"That quack should have his ear nailed to the Tron," McCrae seethed as they walked away.

"He is no different to those who flagellate themselves in the streets to absolve their sins, which apparently brought the plague upon us. I however, do not believe some pastor fornicating with a lady of the night caused this."

"At least they're not robbing folk."

"I am astonished people believe there are such things as unicorns, let alone powdered horns."

"People believe anything when they're afraid."

They stopped by fifteen-year-old redhead lass selling herbs.

McCrae smiled. "Morning Nessie. Is Isabelle not here today?"

"She's helping Marion Gibb with her healing."

James requested some herbs and dropped his coin into the plague stone. Nessie removed the coin and handed James the herbs.

"I only need a small amount, you can have the rest," he told McCrae as they walked away. James tripped over the hen he had accosted. McCrae caught him, laughing. "Buy Katrein something. A scarf or flowers."

"'I'm sorry I failed to save yer parents, here's a scarf to banish yer grief'. It's not a bandage that will heal her wounds."

"My you are a glumbucket today. Fine, buy me a scarf that I can give to a lady."

"You *pay* prostitutes, you don't give them gifts."

"I would not risk the humiliation placed upon me should my master discover I fornicated with a prostitute." James took a blue scarf off the seller and draped it around his neck.

"You look bonny. That blue matches yer eyes."

James dropped a coin into the vinegar then handed the scarf to McCrae.

"Is this a wedding present? Yer father can afford a bigger dowry than that scarf. I demand a top position in the hospital."

"The bride's family pay the dowry, not the groom's."

McCrae laughed. "*You* are the one who wore a dress."

"*Three* men asked for my hand in marriage that night and yet I went home with you."

"You didn't come home with me – I carried you because you were too drunk to walk and nobody would buy you from me."

"Give the scarf to Katrein or I shall wear it every time we are together, even when I am performing surgeries or shaving some man's face. As bonny as I look in it, it will only get covered in blood or chemicals."

McCrae took the scarf. "Maybe I'm marrying the wrong person." He winked.

James put his hand on his heart. "When you turn those twinkling eyes to me, my heart does a wee dance."

"It's called fear." He lifted James's watch, which hung around his neck. "We're late."

They raced each other to the deacon's house, dodging chickens, people and carts. McCrae beat James there. James was still breathless as they took their seats in the front row.

"Promise me you will be careful with the councillors, Alex. Fergusson is a cold-hearted monster."

"I deal with the dying every day. A man in fancy clothing does not frighten me."

"He is dangerous."

"So is the plague. Neither have killed me yet."

Chapter 7

"Can any of these potions make me fly?" Katrein peered into an alembic over a stand in James's lodgings. A flame licked the base of the alembic, the green liquid bubbling gently. Candles filled the room, banishing the dark. "Alex does not want me walking the streets and forbids me from me riding in my cousin's cart. Flying might be safer."

"I told you, you need a broomstick," McCrae said, sitting on the bed beside James, who lay propped against his pillows. "And a black cat."

"I have a potion that makes you *think* you can fly," James replied. "Unfortunately it worked a wee bit too well and my rather foolish test subject flapped his arms and jumped off the Flodden wall shouting 'I'm the birdman of Edinburgh'. I'm sure his broken leg will heal quickly." He tapped the splints keeping his leg immobile. "Alex happened to be passing and came to my rescue. As he lifted me into his strong arms, I nearly swooned."

"I should've left you to be pecked by the crows, taught you a lesson." McCrae leaned over to poke James's leg. James screeched, clutching the splint. "How will you perform surgeries with a broken leg?"

"I'll hire a bonny apprentice. Or I'll buy that hen. She would not scold me as you do." He glanced at the notebook he held. "I am working on an elixir that will help people live longer. One day I hope to eradicate death."

"Promise you won't test them on yerself. You will commit self-murder."

"You are a prophet of doom, Alex. Have faith in science. I refuse to die until I have either an ailment or a cure named after me. I am also creating a potion that will bring people back from the dead."

Katrein smiled. "You said raising the dead was necromancy, Alex. Shame on you. It's science."

"Why would you want corpses walking the streets?"

James smiled. "I'm not allowed to practise on the living so I shall practise on the dead. Once I discover the ingredient that will awaken them from the eternal sleep, I can work on making people live forever. Think of the glorious changes we would witness in this world! In science, medicine, society. We would be heroes, Alex!"

"We would be burned."

"They can burn us, but my elixir ensures we shall not die."

"So we suffer until they chop our heads off."

James shook his head. "Is he a gloom worm with you, Katrein?"

"I find him far more agreeable when he's asleep." She walked over and ran her fingers through McCrae's hair.

"Do you ever study or do you spend yer days drinking potions and leaping off walls?" McCrae picked up an anatomy book and flicked through it. "You'll never pass yer examinations if you don't study. You can experiment on the dead as much as you wish once yer a doctor."

James sighed. "When did you really learn? When you read about human dissection or when you held another man's heart in your hand, having cut it from his body?"

"Being right does not mean yer sane. I'm surrounded by a lass who wishes to raise the dead, a man who thinks he can fly and a man who sees ghosts. Maybe the plague is eating folks' minds."

"Maybe it's you," Katrein teased, squeezing McCrae's shoulders. "Yer the one thing we have in common. I refuse to accept the only sane one dresses as a bird."

He pulled her onto his lap.

"I second that," James said. "Especially when you borrow ideas from the French. When they summon the witch prickers to hunt for our devil's marks, we shall be sure to tell them you are responsible."

"Why does everyone wish to see me tried for witchcraft?" McCrae laughed and pinched Katrein's side, making her wriggle. "Yer pale James, are you unwell?" He leaned forwards and touched James's forehead.

"A mild fever brought on by a broken leg and foolishness."

Katrein fetched scissors and a bowl of water and wiped James's face." May I?" She gestured to his breeches.

"You can do whatever you like to me."

Katrein cut a slit in James's trouser leg and parted it, revealing a large bruise. "It is well set. You should recover without a limp. Though a limp would remind you to be careful."

"I would look splendid with a cane," James mused. "I shall tell people I was wounded in battle."

"I'll fetch a poultice to help with the pain and swelling," McCrae said. "I fear there is nothing I can do for yer sanity."

"There is a fine line between genius and madness."

"I'll visit you tomorrow," Katrein said.

"With a beautiful nurse caring for me, maybe I will delay my healing. Or break my other leg."

McCrae dropped the book in James's lap. "That should keep you from getting bored."

"Or bore me senseless." James shivered. "Tell me, Katrein. How was life in the ludges?"

Katrein found an extra blanket and draped it over James. "Surprisingly pleasant. Everything was clean and the quartermasters made sure everyone was fed. One woman was hanged for stealing infected clothing, but she was beginning to show signs of the pest, so perhaps hanging was a kinder death."

McCrae and Katrein left James alone and stepped onto Niddry Wynd, heading down the slope. Wind whipped their clothes as they linked arms and turned right onto Cowgate.

"Did you visit Margret before you left?" McCrae asked.

"Aye, with the midwife. Margret begged us to deliver her baby." Sorrow crossed her face. "The baby was dead inside her. Margret died as we cut it out. Poor Jim."

They walked in silence.

Katrein hitched her skirts over the mud. "Do you think James will bring the dead back to life?"

"If it was possible, someone would have performed it by now."

"Maybe they have. Maybe they are rotting at the bottom of the Nor' Loch. What about his elixir? Do you think folk can live forever?"

"No. Would you want to live in a world vastly different from this? This city changed beyond recognition? I imagine living forever would get tiresome."

"A world without death, without this horrible pestilence. I would like that."

"You want an army of murderous corpses." He smiled.

"Is it so bad to have ambition?" She prodded his ribs.

"When folk plan for the future, an army of cadavers does not feature in their vision of a home and family."

"They lack my imagination."

A shadow moved up ahead. McCrae raised his lantern, the flame causing grotesque monsters to creep along the tenement walls. A breeze danced past, whispering his name. He looked over his shoulder.

John Petrie stood behind him, his skin decomposing, his eyes milky and bloodshot. He opened his peeling mouth, soil tumbling to the ground.

"McCrae."

Katrein tugged his arm. "Alex?"

He forced himself to smile. "It seems insanity is contagious."

He glanced behind him, his heart thumping. The street was deserted. He tightened his arm around Katrein. An indignant whinny and thundering hooves echoed in the night.

"It's not Hamish," Katrein said. "Bran cannot run that fast."

An empty death cart clattered past, the driver collapsed in the seat. McCrae pulled Katrein out of the way. The cart vanished as it passed them.

"How long has Hamish been seeing ghosts?"

"It started after he nearly drowned when he was a wee lad."

"Does everyone become a ghost?"

"Only those who have met a violent end, or who have unfinished business."

McCrae deepened his voice. "Avenge my foul and most unnatural murder!"

Katrein laughed as they headed right up Old Fishmarket's Close. "I don't think Hamish's ghosts know Shakespeare."

"If I return as a ghost, that's what I would say."

"What if you died naturally?"

"Apparently I would not return."

"I shall be a ghost."

"You believe you will meet a violent end?" He smiled.

"I will play tricks on you and watch you at the washbasin."

"You are wicked."

"That's why I will be a ghost. God hates wicked lasses and the devil would fear me."

They stopped outside Hamish's tenement. McCrae kissed Katrein's lips lightly. She gripped his doublet, pulling him closer. He stumbled, pinning her to the wall as he kissed her passionately. She moaned, wrapping her arms around his neck.

McCrae reluctantly pulled away, breathing hard. It felt wrong to feel so alive when surrounded by so much death. "Goodnight. I'll see you tomorrow." He ran his trembling fingers through her hair.

"Unless I become a ghost. Then I'll see you in the night." Katrein cackled as she opened the door and slipped inside. She waved through the window.

McCrae walked back down towards Cowgate, searching the lonely night. Not even the dead roamed the streets. His breathing became shallow as he reached the spot where Petrie had stood. Scolding himself, he quickened his pace until he reached Candlemaker Row. He hated nights as black as this one, when his lantern was the only light. It felt as though he was trapped in Death's soul. In the dark, ghost stories could be true.

He entered his loft and gathered comfrey leaves and scotch before returning outside. The streets were eerily silent; not even a death cart's bell haunted the city. McCrae's footsteps seemed unnaturally loud, as though the damned marched behind him.

A lone candle burned in James's lodgings. A shadow crossed the window. McCrae bounded up the steps and opened the door. James stood near his worktable, scooping powder into a crucible.

"James!"

James whirled around, spilling the powder. The crucible drowned in a fiery shroud.

"Look what you made me do, Alex."

"You should be in bed."

"I had an idea for an experiment. I cannot rest until I have tested it. Allow me to finish and I will stay tucked up all night, sleeping like the dead." He frowned. "Something's vexing you."

"It's nothing."

"Alex. I know you better than I know myself."

McCrae pulled the comfrey leaves from his pocket and ground them with a pestle and mortar then poured boiling water over them.

James added liquids to his mixture.

McCrae stirred the leaves. "Do you believe in ghosts?"

James glanced up. "Of course not! Who has been filling your head with such thoughts?"

"Hamish sees them." McCrae placed the comfrey mixture in a cloth and folded the ends over.

"Hamish is not exactly of sound mind; the man chooses to ride with the dead."

"I saw Petrie."

James stared at him. "In the pit?"

"In the street. He looked as though he had crawled from the pit. Then he vanished."

"Perhaps your herbs are affecting your mind."

"He said my name."

The liquid turned pink then purple before settling on blue.

"What the devil is that?" McCrae asked.

"My immortality potion."

"You don't believe in ghosts but you believe you can resurrect the dead?"

"Ghosts are superstition. This is science. It can only be proved or disproved."

James picked up the crucible and hobbled to a dead plant on the windowsill. He poured a small amount into the pot then stood back.

McCrae folded his arms. "Bed, James."

"Wait." James checked his watch.

"Bed."

"Don't use your stern voice; it does queer things to people."

McCrae slapped James's arm. "Bed. Or I'll break yer other leg."

"Wait!"

The plant slowly straightened, its withered leaves uncurling. The bowed head rose and opened. McCrae stumbled backwards, his mind refusing to believe what his eyes swore he witnessed.

"I did it!" James gaped at the plant. "One of my experiments actually worked!"

"It's still dead."

"It's alive!"

"It's *dead*."

James gave the plant water. It sank into the soil. "Dead things don't drink."

"It's shrivelled and grey."

"Then I have raised the dead. Katrein will be thrilled."

"This is witchcraft!"

"Nonsense. I have uttered no magic words. And I'm a doctor. It is only witchcraft if you are a witch."

James limped to the bed and climbed in. McCrae lifted James's leg in before undressing him. He placed the comfrey poultice on James's leg then arranged the blankets over him and handed him a glass of scotch.

"Will your betrothed be happy about you undressing a man?"

McCrae laughed and swatted his head. "I have undressed you many times. You were always too drunk to notice."

"I feel so violated! Yet oddly touched."

McCrae circled to the other side of the bed and removed his boots, doublet and shirt. He lay on the bed.

"Do all your patients get special treatment?"

"Only the ones who will try to raise dead plants in their sleep."

McCrae extinguished the lantern. The night claimed the room.

***

McCrae woke, feeling skin beneath his face. He opened his eyes, darkness embracing him. James's heart thumped against his ear. His arm was draped over James's stomach.

"What would Katrein say if she saw you?" James's voice was slurred. He brushed McCrae's hair off his forehead.

"She'd ask you if she could expect a good wedding night." McCrae sat up, James's arm falling off his shoulders.

"Has my plant eaten the other plants?"

McCrae groped for the flint box and struck the flint until a spark fell on the cloth. He coaxed it into life then lit the candle in the lantern. "It's still dead."

"Dead dead or living dead?"

"There's a difference?"

James propped himself up on the pillows and winced. McCrae turned, the lantern casting fiery shadows onto James. McCrae froze, his heart feeling as though Death gripped it in his bony hand.

"You look as though I really have raised the dead."

McCrae opened his mouth, but no words escaped. He touched James's chest. James glanced down and swore.

Pale red roses decorated his skin.

Chapter 8

Shadows chased McCrae through the wynds, his feet slipping in the filth. Without his lantern, the streets were blacker than the devil's heart. Even the moon had forsaken Edinburgh. Water splashed his bare chest, his doublet hanging open. The bells on the death carts sounded mocking in their musical tinkling, like Death playing a song for the last dance.

"Bring out yer dead!"

Words that had become the city's motto now shot fear into his heart. Those words would not be his last memory of James when he laid his rotting corpse in a cart.

He could not run fast enough. His treacherous legs forgot how to climb the stairs as he stumbled up to his room. He crashed through his door, his heart pounding.

Through a blurred veil of tears, he saw his costume waiting on the bed. Stripping off his clothes, he fell onto his bed in an effort to tug off his boots while walking. He dressed in the costume, closing his eyes as he fastened the mask. Tears slid down his cheeks. He raised the hood. He was no longer James's friend.

He was Death.

McCrae grabbed his herbs, lance and stick and left, the door banging shut. His cloak billowed as he tore through the streets, jumping over rats that seemed determined to trip him.

"Gardyloo!"

"Shit!" McCrae dived into a doorway and pressed against the door. "Ten o'clock was hours ago!"

The shower passed in front of him, splashing his boots. The stench of waste and rotting vegetables turned his stomach. He ducked out of the doorway, leapt over the puddle and ran to James's lodgings. Sweat trickled down his skin, mingling with his tears.

James stood by his potions, heating a flask. He had dressed, but left his shirt unbuttoned. The lantern stood open, having sacrificed its flame to the candles.

"You should be resting." McCrae hated the way his voice quivered.

James jumped, touching his chest. "Are you trying to scare me into my grave?" He returned his attention to his flask. "I will rest in my coffin."

McCrae squeezed James's shoulder. "James—"

"How long from the disease presenting itself until the patient dies?"

McCrae's throat burned. He rested his forehead on the back of James's head, his beak hanging down James's back. "Don't speak of it."

"How long?"

McCrae swallowed and raised his head, his hand slipping down James's back in defeat. "Three days. Four at the most. Two if yer lucky."

"All the more reason not to rest. If I am going to have a potion named after me, I have three days to achieve it." James sprinkled powder into the flask, stepping back when vapour spiralled from it.

McCrae glanced in the mirror behind the table. He looked like a spectre of Death, come to claim James's soul.

McCrae unbuckled his mask and pushed it up, wiping his eyes with his arm. "Potions are not supposed to do that."

James cocked his head. "Do you hear that?"

THE MALIGNANT DEAD

Gentle ticking caressed McCrae's ears. The longer he listened, the louder it became.

"The death watch beetle predicts I will die. We must work quickly."

"You believe that superstition?" McCrae shuddered as the ticking continued. He pulled James's phial of green liquid from his pocket.

"That was my error! I stopped drinking that." James tapped McCrae's phial. "I created a new potion that tasted sweeter. Clearly it was not as effective."

McCrae watched James working, picturing the rose pattern blooming on his chest, the pus and decay his other patients suffered. He would not die like them. He could not help James if he was infected too. He drank the potion. He gagged but forced it down until the phial was empty.

"Let me treat you."

"Alex, I have enough potions to heal myself of every disease known to man. And some man does not know about yet." James added a herb to the flask, poured it into a goblet then turned around. He raised the goblet of blue liquid. "To immortality!"

"If you imagine you can fly again, I'll tie you to yer bed until the plague has taken you."

"Ooh promises." James smiled playfully, waggling one eyebrow. "Fancy a taste? I mixed it with that concoction I gave the plant."

"The plant is dead."

"You have no love for romance."

McCrae took the goblet and grimaced. "Could you make something that does not smell like my patients?"

"There are three things you must suffer for: beauty, love and science."

"Nothing is worth suffering for."

James smiled. "How wrong you are. Drink."

"I'm appeasing a sick man. I don't believe yer mad potions will work. To vomiting over yer floor!" McCrae toasted James and drank. He spluttered. "Now get into bed."

McCrae helped James into bed then placed leeches on his body.

James winced. "Must you place these vile creatures on me?"

"They will drink the plague from yer blood." McCrae hung herbs by the bed then fetched a bowl of water.

"Are you hoping to wash the plague from me? I fear this will change our friendship into one of an unspeakable love."

"Stop drinking yer damn potions and reading poetry. I'm certain the filth that consumes Edinburgh is assisting the plague's survival. If dirt gets into a wound, it becomes infected and sometimes, the limb must be removed. Think what dirt can do to those weakened by plague. Leith's quartermasters are paying female prisoners or women from infected families to clean their streets. There are not enough men alive in Leith to help. It's perilous work. My theory is not as mad as the council believe."

"Will you take a broom to Edinburgh? I can see you in that costume, cleaning the streets like the servants cleaning my castle."

McCrae wrung out the cloth and wiped it along James's chest. "You should have gone to London and continued yer work, become as famous as you've always dreamed of being."

"You talk like I won't survive." James shivered. "What kind of man would I be if I left my best friend to die alone?"

"A sane one. A *healthy* one."

"A disloyal one. You are prepared to risk your life helping pestilent strangers, the least I could do is stay in Edinburgh to be there for you. Of course I did not foresee I would get sick. Other people's mortality is easier to believe than your own. I was going to be the greatest apothecary the world has ever known. People would pay ridiculous prices for a small phial of my latest potion. Women would shed their clothes and morals for one night with me in exchange for my ageing cure."

"I can fetch a whore from the inn. Although they now flee when they see me."

"Work is more important than love. It will never break my heart or give me syphilis."

McCrae prised the leeches off James and returned them to the box.

James coughed. "Hand me that phial of purple liquid."

McCrae fetched the phial. "Drinking anything this colour cannot be good for you."

"Neither is the plague." James removed the cork and took a sip. He offered it to McCrae.

He sniffed the phial then took a tentative sip. "What does this do?"

"Absolutely no idea. But we can find out together. One last adventure. Hand me my notebook. I must record everything."

McCrae fetched the notebook, a quill and an inkpot. "I won't allow you to die, James. Who will stand by me at my wedding? Who will stop me punching councillors?"

James patted McCrae's cheek. "Don't worry. With all these potions inside me, I will either live forever or wake from death as a putrid gargoyle, and terrorise the city."

"I would love to see a putrid gargoyle eating the councillors and chasing peasants. Yer name would certainly be remembered then. 'James Lowther: doctor, friend, monster'."

"Says the man in the beak."

"I'll send word to yer father."

"He could not bear the shame of his favourite son–"

McCrae laughed. "Yer not his favourite!"

"–his favourite son dying like the peasants."

"He dumped you in Edinburgh whilst yer brothers are in London."

"He invited me to work in Bedlam with him. I refused."

"Why?"

"You would not have accompanied me. I was placed here to be your guardian angel. Without you, who would stand by me whilst I make my latest potion? Who would stop me punching my father?"

"You have never thrown a punch in yer life!"

"It's never too late to start. Right, we have three days to figure out why you of all people haven't caught this wretched disease. I have seen you carrying their pestilent bodies to the cart, yet you are not afflicted. Petrie died within a week. What are you doing differently?"

"Petrie didn't wear my costume. He relied on a rabbit's foot and quack remedies."

"I have never understood charms. How is a rabbit foot lucky? It wasn't lucky for the rabbit." James rubbed his cheek as he studied McCrae's costume. "Perhaps your dirt theory is correct. Your costume prevents dirt infecting you."

"The herbs in my beak banish the smell and stop me inhaling it if it's airborne."

"What if the plague isn't contagious?"

"Disease cannot spread this fast without being contagious."

"It could be in the water, the food. The terrible crops over winter cannot help – famine is rife and people are too weak to fight pestilence. Maybe the trade ships brought the plague from a far-off land and that is why Leith has suffered more deaths. Their docks are where the ships come in. You've lain by me all night. If you don't display symptoms by tomorrow, it cannot be contagious. Did you know there was an outbreak of the plague almost exactly three hundred years ago? They called it the Black Death. It killed twenty five million people in Europe. Why did it not kill everyone?"

"Maybe folk fled, like they're doing now."

"Perhaps some people cannot catch it. What if it's not your costume, but something in your blood that keeps you healthy? Allow me to take some blood."

"Will you rest if I agree?"

James pointed to his worktable. McCrae removed his gloves then fetched a needle and a crucible. James pricked McCrae's fingertip and squeezed the blood into the crucible. He sent McCrae to fetch another then handed McCrae the needle. McCrae stabbed James's finger. His blood dripped into the crucible.

"I'll combine our blood, see if mine infects yours," James said as McCrae wrote their names on parchment and placed the crucibles on the correct names.

"Knowing you, we'll create a bairn." McCrae returned to the bed.

"With your looks and my wit and intelligence, our baby would be king!"

McCrae laughed. "It might have *yer* looks and *my* intelligence then it would be shot. Or spend its days hiding in the rafters of St Giles and nights roaming the streets, feasting on the blood and flesh of the living."

"The legend of James McCrae or Alex Lowther will live for centuries in books and plays, terrifying generations to come. My father would be *delighted*. He begs me to provide him with a grandchild, even though my brothers have already given him three. Because I am his favourite."

"Or because he believes a bairn would stop you drinking potions."

"I cannot stop. Genius is a sip away. If your blood remains uninfected then you're the cure. I shall drain the blood from my body and replace it with yours."

"Nobody has successfully performed that procedure."

"We could be the first! Our names will be remembered throughout history. And not because of the monstrous child we produced."

"If it keeps you alive, I'll try it."

"You'll die."

"But you'll live. You will become the greatest apothecary man the world has ever known. Folk need that. They don't need a linen seller in a scary costume."

"*I* do. A life without you is no life at all."

McCrae smiled and plucked a lock of hair from James's forehead. He smoothed it back. "Don't ever die on me, James."

"I'm doing my best."

"Let me listen to yer heart." McCrae placed his ear against James's chest. His heartbeat was loud and swift. He could not imagine the day it would not beat.

"It is up to the Fates when they cut my mortal coil. I wish to be buried in a mausoleum in Gray-friar. A grand one with elaborate carvings, to show future generations what a successful doctor I was. Nothing too lavish."

"I'll erect railings around it."

"Whatever for?"

"To stop you climbing out and eating people. Perhaps I should stake you and cut off yer head."

"Harsh, Alex. You would not want a visit from your oldest friend?" James pushed McCrae upright.

"You'll probably awaken as the blood-drinking undead."

"I hope not. Blood has a foul taste. And it would stain my clothes. Do not engrave the cause of death on my mausoleum. I wish to be remembered as the doctor who died from one of his experiments, where people would think me insane now, but in years to come will hail me a genius. I don't want to be tossed into one of those wretched pits like a peasant. My corpse would blush until my face falls off."

McCrae gripped James's hand, his eyes burning with the tears he would not allow himself to shed. "If you commit self-murder with yer potions, you'll be buried under crossroads to stop yer spirit from wandering."

James reached under his pillow and handed McCrae a white handkerchief. "Put it in the window when you leave. I suppose you must have a searcher paint one of those ghastly crosses on my door. It grieves me the peasants will know I'm not invincible. I suppose even gods have to die."

McCrae smiled sadly and left James's rooms, lowering his mask. Dawn had forced its way through the night's impenetrable cloak. Paint dribbled down the door of a tenement opposite. A shaking hand pushed a white rag out of the window. McCrae walked across the street and knocked on the door, pocketing James's handkerchief.

Chapter 9

The gallows creaked. Muffled gurgling came from the man who kicked and twitched on the end of his rope. Veins in his eyes burst, his lips turning blue. He frantically tried freeing his hands, which were bound behind his back. Bloodied nail gouges stained his skin.

"Help...me." His words were choked from his throat, sounding more like a rasp than a plea for mercy.

The councillors stood on the second storey extension on the west side of the Old Tolbooth. The roof was flat, the gallows protruding from the wall. Ketch stood silently to the side, his big arms folded across his broad chest. Doctor Sampson stood beside him. A month ago a crowd of ten thousand would have gathered in Lawnmarket below, or watched from their tenements. Now the silence was eerie, the crowd's cheers nothing more than ghosts echoing through the deserted streets.

"It's a shame people are missing this." Fergusson stared at the large cloths blocking the public's view of the execution. "It might remind them failing to report an infection has consequences."

"Executions were good family entertainment," Douglas said. "The baker profited with his execution biscuits. The rope maker sold miniature nooses by the dozen. Edinburgh needs the money from outsiders who visited for the spectacle. I remember my first execution when I was a wee laddie. I had never seen a criminal before. It's a shame it's come to this."

"I'm not comfortable with this level of punishment for failure to report an infection," Kilbride said.

"Branding them did not deter them," Fergusson said.

"Soon there will be more people buried under Edinburgh than living in it."

"Chances are these people are already diseased. We are giving them a quicker, kinder death and stopping the spread of the plague. We must be seen to be punishing criminals. Do you want this city becoming a lawless society; thieves, murderers, rapists running riot?"

"No, but this man is a cartwright, not a criminal."

"By not reporting his wife's infection, he risked many lives, because they were both able to walk the streets, endangering more people. He is a murderer as much as the man who knifes people in the wynds. He deserves to hang. It is better for one man to die than a hundred."

"Can we not pull on his legs?"

"No. Give him time to make his peace with God."

Guttural groaning came from the man's swollen throat. Fergusson lifted his watch and glanced at the face. He sighed and folded his arms. The man spasmed before hanging still. His leg twitched. Fergusson signalled to Sampson, who examined him and declared him dead.

"Cut him down and deliver him to the deacon. At least these hangings are providing the students with learning materials. They are demanding more than we can supply. It's a shame we cannot sell them plague victims. They would be more useful to the students than to the gravedigger."

The councillors returned inside to their offices in the tower. The smell of bergamot and burning brimstone greeted them. Fergusson shuddered. This was what Hell would smell like.

"As bodies are becoming scarce for the deacon, we should charge him," Douglas said. "Criminals are dying from the plague, rather than the noose. We would raise a handsome amount charging a shilling per corpse."

"I agree," Kilbride said. "With trade restrictions in place, he will have no choice but to pay."

Fergusson nodded. "Excellent idea. We will use the money to revive Edinburgh once the plague has been cured. The dead can pay for the living."

Douglas dipped his quill into his inkpot and wrote on a clean sheet.

Knocking echoed through the room. A beaked, cloaked figure strode in. Fergusson froze before realising it was the plague doctor. He would never get used to that nightmare-inducing costume. He was certain McCrae wore it not to protect himself, but to frighten everyone around him. He probably named himself 'Doctor Death' and enjoyed the fear he created.

"You cannot charge in here without making an appointment," Fergusson snapped. "This is not your home."

"About my wage…" McCrae's voice was muffled.

Fergusson clasped his hands. "Remove that hideous mask, McCrae. You are not amongst the diseased."

McCrae lowered his hood and unbuckled the mask. His hair clung to his forehead. Dark circles haunted his bloodshot eyes, as though the ashes of the dead stained them. When McCrae started the duty, he had looked younger than his twenty-six years. It seemed each life he failed to save added one year to him.

"You've been promising to pay me for four weeks."

"You will be paid once this…pestilence is cured. How many times must I tell you this? Clearly the deacon does not teach you to listen, only to carve up the dead."

"I need to buy herbs and pay for my wedding to Katrein."

"Have her parents not paid you a dowry?"

"I put her parents on the death cart four weeks ago."

"That is...unfortunate, but the terms were clear." Fergusson pressed a cloth to his face to cover the odour of pus, decay, sweat and the sweet smell of herbs and tobacco that wafted around McCrae. Perhaps he was what Hell smells like. Maybe they could hang him simply for smelling bad. The deacon would likely pay extra to dissect one of his apprentices. Seeing how long McCrae had survived, they could charge a large sum for his corpse. The secret to curing the plague could lie within this ruffian's blood.

"I have no money. With the lack of trade, herbs and tobacco are becoming expensive."

Fergusson's eyes narrowed. He'd appeal to his conscience. That would get rid of him. "Soon Scotland will be filled with corpses and ghosts. Saving the city is more important than your wedding night."

"*I'm* not the one hanging the healthy! How many rich folk have danced on the end of the noose? None. You allowed them to flee, taking the plague with them."

"The gates are locked. Nobody is allowed to flee."

"You locked them *after* the rich had fled. Do the poor not deserve the same treatment?"

"The poor are being treated in the ludges and are faring rather well." Fergusson leaned forwards, fixing McCrae with a steely glare. "Do you have any other business or did you come here to tell us how to perform our roles? Because you're clearly not fulfilling *yours*."

McCrae's hands curled into fists. Fergusson waited. If McCrae struck him, he would have McCrae thrown in the Tolbooth. There were plenty of reasons to hang a man. He only needed one.

"I'm risking my *life*. I cannot save folk if I cannot buy herbs to treat them!"

"Lower your voice. You are in council offices, not brawling with your friends in the inn. You will show us respect or you will leave."

"I have done *everything* you asked, including treating the sick in their homes. Everyone I have known my entire life is *dying*. You want to save Edinburgh, *you* treat the sick."

"We are not qualified doctors."

"Neither am I."

"You are entitled to the dead's possessions, same as the clengers. Do you hear *them* complaining about their wage?"

"No, you've paid them. I'd rather starve than rob the dead. I may be losing those I love, but I will not lose my morals."

"Then return next week when you have found your decorum."

"By next week, the only coin I'll have will be the one I use to pay the devil when I enter his gates." McCrae slapped the mask against his leg.

The mask was more terrifying by itself, as though it could come to life and maul them like some creature from ancient superstitions. Its glassy eyes had seen too much death. Fergusson imagined anyone who wore it would be forced to witness its nightmares.

"Folk would be horrified to learn from the town crier they're dying because it's cheaper to bury the dead than save the living. They will call for yer heads. You had better pray when yer families catch the plague, I have enough herbs to treat them."

Fergusson sat up straighter and glowered. "Are you *threatening* us, you insufferable wretch?"

"No. But the plague cannot be cured with unicorn horns and empty promises."

McCrae marched out, a trail of muddy prints following him, as though Death walked in his shadow. The door banged, the building shaking. Fergusson scowled. He fought for his seat on the council. He would not lose it to a man dressed as a bird.

"We were foolish offering that wage," Douglas murmured. "Once he realises we cannot pay him, we are done for."

"Offering a low wage would leave us without a doctor," Fergusson said. "He will not tell the town crier. Who would listen to him? He is the son of a market trader with grand ideas about being a doctor. People are scared of him."

"They might not listen to *him*, but they would listen to his friend, James Lowther. *He* is the son of an eminent doctor in London and one of the richest men in Edinburgh."

"The Lowther lad is full of fanciful ideas. He spends too long with his potions. He is the only wealthy person who has remained here. That is the sign of insanity. Nobody listens to the insane. And he is English. Everyone hates the English."

"McCrae could leave us insolvent if we pay him, or ruin us if we don't," Kilbride said. "We should pay him a small amount."

"And reward his greed and audacity?"

Uneasy silence settled over the room. Douglas stared at the sheet in front of him whilst Kilbride fidgeted with his fingers.

Fergusson eyed the footprints, rage festering in his gut. The plague was not the only way to kill a man.

Chapter 10

The corpse's skin yielded to the blade's touch. McCrae peeled the skin off the man's bones to expose his inner workings. Bloodied ribs encased the heart; a jail cell made from bones.

"Are you hoping to find the secret of life amongst the bloody remains of a criminal?" James asked, entering the loft.

"Katrein wishes to know where the soul is located. I think…" McCrae groped in the man's body. "…it's near the kidneys."

"I always thought it was in the liver. There's plenty of room for it. If a woman's body can harbour a baby, perhaps it's not so impossible to believe a soul can fit in there. Did Gregor ask why you wanted another corpse?"

"I took him from the pit when Gregor was in the inn."

"Alex! You will be caught."

"Folk are used to seeing me carrying dead bodies. If I understand how the plague spreads, perhaps I can stop it. If you don't agree with stealing corpses, why did you pay for them?"

"Friends do not let friends swing on the gallows alone."

McCrae pulled his blood-soaked hands free. "You should be in bed."

James waved his hand dismissively. "I never tire of watching you plunge your hands inside a man's innards. I cannot believe I allow you to treat me after I have witnessed you remove a man's bowel from his cold body."

"Better a cold body than a warm one. Less screaming."

"Will Katrein will let you touch her after you've been groping some man's bladder?"

"I know how to use a washbasin." McCrae flicked his fingers at him. A blood drop spattered McCrae's boot.

"Seeing a body opened like a treasure chest makes me question God's vision. Why make something so disgusting?" James's face crinkled as he peered into the body.

"For a man who should have died days ago, yer looking remarkably healthy."

"I told you, I will live forever. For someone who's slept beside the pestilent every night, you're remarkably healthy."

"Perhaps I *am* the devil, like my patients believe. They say I'm the plague doctor not because I *treat* the illness, but because I *bring* it."

"God would never bestow that much power upon you. The quiet ones are the most dangerous."

"I believe yer potions have created a different strain of plague. You have no buboes."

"It will be known as the Lowther Plague. Deadly, but free from pus."

"You wish to give yer name to a foul disease?"

"My name *will* live on, even if it is in something which inspires terror. In years to come, your costume will be known as the McCrae. We shall both create nightmares."

"Are yer potions making you sick? What is in them?
"Arsenic. And hemlock."

"James! Yer poisoning yerself!"

"Poisons have curing properties too."

"They are dangerous."

"So is the plague."

James leaned on his cane and hobbled around the table, catching his splinted leg on a chair. He shivered and pulled his coat tighter around him. Dull skin stretched over his cheekbones. His hat was pulled down to his eyes. Thick gloves covered his bony hands, hiding the red roses from anyone who came close enough to notice.

"You will not find the cure for the plague inside this man's kidney. The cure lies in my flasks and my curious mind."

"I administered yer latest potion to one of our fellow students, Clyde – with his consent. He's had the plague three days, yet isn't as ill as the others. You've created something that is fighting it."

James removed a glove and proffered his hand. "Kiss me, I'm a genius."

McCrae mockingly kissed his ring. "You've survived longer than anyone else. Maybe because you don't live amongst filth and you can buy food."

"Must you steal my glory? Admit I'm a genius and I'm curing the plague. Now I will definitely have a potion named after me. 'A drop of Lowther cures all ills'. Maybe they will open a school of apothecary – The James Lowther Institute. That way, even if I die, I will still live forever."

"If they're naming anything after you, it will be dying after trying a dangerous experiment." He imitated James's English accent. "Why I do believe this patient committed an act of Lowthering, thereby causing his death."

"Why am I friends with you? You break my heart every day. I must be atoning for sinful thoughts."

McCrae cackled. "God does not punish thoughts."

"Just as well. I would be damned a thousand times over."

"As would I. Fortunately I can only be damned for the unholy act of removing a body from its grave. I need to test yer potion on more patients. It's hard convincing them to agree. I don't know if it's the potion that scares them, or me. Rest assured, if they become cannibals, I will be sure to tell the council who is responsible."

"They would not hang a dying man."

"They would. Then they'd sell yer body to the deacon so we can cut you up in class."

"I'm not dying on the end of a noose. It's undignified. They do not name institutes after people who dance the hangman's jig." James examined a jar containing an appendix. "At least promise to pickle my brain in a jar so in years to come, people will marvel at the size of it."

"I'll put it in yer smallest crucible, next to yer loins. Though the visitors would need a microscope for that."

James tapped McCrae's ankle with his cane. "Alex, it is improper to admire another man's loins, let alone pickle them in jars. Terrible things will be said about you. You'll die like Edward II. The shadow of your shame will be cast over me and they will deem me too handsome, find me guilty of the same crime and behead me at the Mercat Cross. Is that what you want? My head in a basket like loaves of bread?"

"Why would you be beheaded whilst I die with a poker inserted into my arse?"

"Don't be vulgar, Alex. Noblemen die by the axe."

"Apart from Edward II."

"He was murdered, not executed. To be executed for that crime would involve being strangled at the stake then burned. Like a witch." He put the jar down. "How have you explained my absence to the deacon?"

"I told him you drank another of yer potions, thought yer good leg had to come to life so struck it with a hammer to kill it."

"You made me sound *insane*?"

"The fact he believed me proves you *are* insane."

"*Peasants* are insane. Rich people are *eccentric*."

McCrae cracked open the corpse's ribs then placed his hands and blade inside the body and cut out the heart. He lifted it out.

"Ah the heart. The one part of our body that causes so much pain." James sighed, poking it. "The Greeks were correct in their belief Eros was dangerous. His arrows are poison, causing nothing but madness and grief if the heart cannot have what it yearns for."

"Or if his arrow severs the heart in two." McCrae sliced the heart and held up both halves. "The heart is merely an instrument to pump blood around the body. Unless I misread William Harvey's text."

James shook his head. "I have looks, money, charm, wit, intelligence and romance. Explain how *you* won the fair Katrein's heart?"

"She saw me shirtless after you tripped me in the mud."

James banged his cane on the floor. "Damn my playful nature!"

McCrae smiled. "She was already promised to me, but it was gazing upon me shirtless that made her love me."

"My father has arranged for me to be wed four times. I have successfully averted all of them."

"How?"

"Whenever I am to meet their fathers, one of my experiments happens to explode. No man wishes for his daughter to marry a mad man."

McCrae laughed. "Were their dowries not sufficient?"

"On the contrary. I was offered positions in hospitals in Paris and Rome. But I shall only marry for love."

"Love does not happen immediately. It's like a disease. It takes time to fester and grow."

James consulted his pocket watch. "Time to become a ghost in this city." He limped to the door. He turned. "Where is that white rag I gave you?"

"I used it to clean pus from my patients." McCrae removed a lung and examined it.

"That was my silk handkerchief!"

"You can have it back if you wish."

"I should have been locked in."

"The streets are lonely enough."

"Why is there no cross on my door?"

McCrae placed the lung in a dish on another table.

James's voice softened. "They will hang you."

McCrae gripped the table. "Every day I risk my life for strangers. What kind of friend would I be if I won't risk it for you? The council will hang me anyway. This way I can die with honour. Go, before yer discovered. We cannot cure the plague from the gallows."

"We would have to wait until they cut us down. Then we would rise from our graves like gods."

"They would not call us gods."

The door clicked shut as McCrae freed the other lung and set it in the dish beside its partner. A rasping moan pierced the silence. He turned around.

The corpse's fingers moved.

McCrae jumped back, dishes clattering as his quivering hands knocked them. The heart spilled its blood over his fingers. The corpse lay still, its chest cavity hacked open, a ring of purple roses around his neck. McCrae checked the pulse in the wrist. Still. He picked up the hand and dropped it. It smacked the table.

"I've been drinking too many of James's potions."

He swiftly cut out the other organs. The quicker he could perform surgery, the less a patient would suffer. The silence felt eerie, like it concealed secrets not meant for the ears of the living. As he removed the small intestine, he was struck by an image of it as a bloody noose brought from the land of the dead to hang those in the land of living, in the judgement courts of Hell.

***

Hamish stopped his cart at the pit. Soon a new one would have to be dug. There was no sign of Gregor. Maybe he was in the inn, drowning the horror from his memory. Hamish tipped the cart, patting Bran's nose as the bodies fell into the pit.

"Ring a ring of roses, a pocketful of posies. Ashes, ashes, we all fall down." Bran flattened his ears. "My singing's not that bad, laddie. You should hear me after I have been downing the ale." He righted the cart and raised his leg to climb up to the seat.

Something groaned.

He lowered his leg and turned around.

Nothing moved in the kirkyard.

A rustle sounded from behind him. Bran's ears rose and swivelled forwards. Hamish cursed under his breath.

"Perhaps the birdman is right and it's in my head."

Shuffling feet moved closer.

Gripping the reins, he turned around. The dead rose from the pit, their limbs stiff as though they had forgotten how to work. Moonlight cast an eerie shroud over their dying skin. They lumbered towards him.

"Hamish."

"Shit!" He backed into his cart.

The dead lurched towards him, their milky eyes sending shivers crawling through his body. His heart galloped. He scrambled into the cart and glanced over his shoulder. More of the dead escaped the pit. The cart bounced over the uneven ground as Bran cantered towards the gate, whinnying. Hamish fought to stay in the seat. He didn't want to be thrown to the mercy of the wandering dead.

Hamish urged Bran on. His hooves rang off the cobblestone as they emerged on the darkened street and raced down the curved slope of Candlemaker Row, sounding like Death's carriage racing over a road of bones.

THE MALIGNANT DEAD

As they reached the corner of Grassmarket, an army of the dead surged towards him, led by a cloaked figure in a beaked mask.

Bran reared, neighing shrilly. The cart tipped and Hamish fell, haunted by the image of falling to the cobbles, his blood slipping between the stones.

He sat up in bed, sweat clinging to him. Darkness swarmed, the monsters creeping closer with each laboured breath. Bran's terrified whinny and galloping hooves chased him into the waking world.

Katrein rushed in, her candle casting evil shadows on the wall and disturbing the two barrowmen he shared the room with. "Hamish! Are you ill?"

"The nightmare visited me."

"You screamed."

"The nightmare does not bring dreams of sunshine and rainbows, Kat." He wiped his face.

Katrein sat on the edge of his bed. "What did she bring you?"

"I don't remember."

She frowned. "Perhaps that's best. Any dream that makes you scream like a lass about to give birth is not a dream you want to remember."

"I didn't scream." He poked her leg.

"You did! I thought I'd find a lass with blood around her feet and a baby in her arms. I nearly grabbed my nurse's bag."

Hamish laughed and smoothed Katrein's unruly hair. "You look as though you've been fighting demons whilst being dragged backwards through woodland. Does Doctor Death know he'll go to sleep with a princess and wake with a gorgon?"

She laughed and slapped his arm. "You monster! Goodnight cousin. May yer dreams be sweeter."

She kissed his forehead then walked out, leaving the candle by his bed. Hamish shivered and pulled his blankets around him. Every time he closed his eyes, he saw the man in the mask, surrounded by his army of the dead.

Chapter 11

"Doctor Death!"

McCrae dodged the bairn's flailing limbs as she writhed as though possessed by a demon. The fire matched her movements, its hungry flames reaching to devour her sweat-slicked skin.

"Hold her still," McCrae told her mother. Sweat slithered down his back. He longed to escape so he could remove his mask and feel the July wind on his face.

"Stay still, Alesonne, the doctor wants to treat you."

Alesonne sank her teeth into his gloves. McCrae bit his tongue, swallowing his curse. He rested his ear against Alesonne's chest.

"No!" She struck the mask.

McCrae pulled away and sighed, readjusting the mask. He should demand a wage increase for dealing with bairns. They could not be reasoned with. Though the council refused to pay the money they promised him; they would not increase it.

"I must lance the bubo under yer arm. The more you move, the more it will hurt."

"I hate you!" She shrieked; a deafening wail which pierced his brain.

The burning witches screamed less.

"She's scared," her mother said.

She'd be more scared when the disease took hold. He blinked away the sweat stinging his eyes. If he didn't leave soon, he would die of the heat, never mind the plague. All that would remain would be a melted pile of leather and the damn mask.

Katrein entered the room. "Allow me."

"You should be outside." McCrae ground his teeth. He didn't need to battle two headstrong lasses.

"People heard the screams and think yer murdering the sick." Katrein knelt beside Alesonne. "May I?"

The mother released Alesonne, who rose to her knees to escape. Katrein rolled her onto her back, wrapped her legs around Alesonne's, and trapped Alesonne's arms with hers.

"Now, Alex."

McCrae wedged a stick in Alesonne's mouth then lanced the bubo under her arm. She screamed, the stick rolling onto the floor. McCrae cleaned up the pus and blood then fetched the poker from the hearth and held it to the wound. Alesonne tried struggling but failed. Katrein wrinkled her nose at the smell of burning flesh and pus.

Tears matted Alesonne's limp hair to her scarlet face. "I hate you!"

"Everyone does," Katrein said. "But he really is lovely."

"Drink this." McCrae held out a phial. "It's yarrow and water. It will help yer fever."

"No!"

"Alesonne, that's a magic potion made by a unicorn," Katrein told her. "The unicorns are good friends of Doctor McCrae's."

"I don't want it!"

"Then we'll give it to another wee lass and she'll visit the unicorns in yer place." Katrein released her.

Alesonne snatched the phial and drank it. She spat. Katrein stood, shaking out her skirt. McCrae handed

THE MALIGNANT DEAD

Alesonne's mother herbs and tobacco then he and Katrein left. A searcher painted a cross on the door.

"You were marvellous," McCrae said as they walked along Cowgate then turned left up Blair Street. He tore his mask off, closing his eyes as the wind kissed his face. He shivered pleasurably as it slipped down his back.

"Bairns are like councillors — they respond well to bribes. I have known the family a while. Every time I treat Alesonne I leave with bruises, scratches and teeth marks. I'm certain my patients think I wrestle bears. I nearly suggested they tie her to the bed and gag her, but that would not look favourably upon me."

McCrae laughed. "I don't know what to do with bairns. Maybe it will be God's will that we do not have them."

"Having seen women give birth, it's not something I wish to suffer. We should raise hens instead."

"We could sell the eggs. We could not sell our bairns."

Katrein giggled.

"I think James's cure is working. One of my fellow students, Clyde, tested the potion after catching the plague a week ago. He's still alive."

"That's wonderful! You must tell the council about yer research!"

"I don't think folk would be happy if we tested these potions on the sick with no knowledge of the effects. We could turn them into flesh-eating monsters whose legend will be so horrific, writers will spend centuries creating plays and books from their crimes."

"Ask the council if you can test it on prisoners. It is better they die helping with yer research than on the end of a noose. Some of them are probably already flesh-eating monsters."

"Once I step foot inside the Tolbooth, Fergusson will lock me in."

"Hamish, James, Bran and I will mount a daring rescue and spirit you away on the eve of yer execution." Katrein imitated flicking reins and galloping up the street.

McCrae raised his eyebrows as she returned to him. "Why not the night of my capture?"

"A daring rescue that will be talked of for centuries through books and plays cannot be planned in an hour. The eve of yer execution gives it more danger."

"In the meantime I would rot."

"We could save you on the gallows if you would prefer."

"None of you are good with a bow and arrow."

"I could tie rope to the top of St Giles and swing across to the Tolbooth, a sword between my teeth."

McCrae laughed and stopped at another house with a red cross on the door. He put his mask on and raised his hood. The mask was cold and slick from his sweat. He entered the house, treated the man then stepped outside, surprised to see Katrein waiting.

"I can help with yer patients. Hold down the difficult ones and charm the handsome ones."

"You'll help me more by not catching the plague."

"Test the potion on me, see if it stops me catching it."

"I'd never forgive myself if it poisoned you or made you think you could fly, like James. It would break my heart to chop yer head off, should you become a snarling beast."

Katrein snarled at him, forming her fingers into talons.

"If you want to help, wear my mask."

"You want folk willing to test it; I am no different to anyone else." She stood on her toes and planted a kiss on the mask's cheek. "If I don't catch it after drinking this, you can give it to everyone. Then Edinburgh can stop dying." She raised the phial, removed the cork then twirled away and drank it. She retched. "Tell James to make it sweeter."

"What have you *done*?" McCrae stared at the empty phial. Nausea pummelled his stomach. "You don't know what it could do to you!" He wanted to reach inside her and drain the liquid from her body.

"Neither would anyone else who drank it. Every day you jeopardise yer life to save folk. James makes potions to save them. I will not watch this city die. If drinking James's mad creations is the only way I can help then so be it. If I die, please make up a heroic tale for my tombstone. I don't want to be known as the lass who died from foolishness, or James and I will have matching epitaphs. Don't let that be my shame." She smiled. "This is a scary time to be alive, Alex. Every day we risk catching this wretched plague and dying in agony, our skin rotting on our bodies, our loved ones watching helplessly as we cough so much blood we drown in it. *Never* let me die that way. *Promise* me, if I catch it, you will end my life."

"I won't murder you, Katrein. And I won't let you die from the plague."

She walked backwards away from him as they reached High Street. "We can either die screaming in our own decomposing skin or–" she waved the phial, "we can die heroes."

She gathered her skirts and ran to the house of her next patient, blowing him a kiss as she disappeared inside. His heart ached and his stomach churned at the thought of losing her, either to the potion or the plague. He could not bear to see her suffer but he could not take a second from her life. He would gladly give his life to spare hers.

Hooves clopped behind him. A bell rang almost in time with the hooves.

"What has my wayward cousin done now?"

Bran nudged McCrae in the back with his nose. He moved to pat the pony. Bran threw his head up, his ears flattened, his teeth bared.

"She drank one of James's potions."

"Why the devil would she do that? That laddie is insane."

"Rich people are eccentric."

"The only difference between the rich and the poor is the rich think they're better than us. But they bleed, piss and die like the rest of us."

"The potion may stop the healthy from catching the infection."

"If she climbs to the top of the Tolbooth and declares she can fly, I'll drive my cart beneath to catch her." Hamish chuckled. "She'd get a shock to land amongst the corpses!"

McCrae smiled. "You look unwell."

Hamish raised his hand. "I don't have the plague and I won't drink Lowther's potions. One of us must keep their sanity, even if the rest of you are throwing yers away."

"Something is vexing you."

"Half the city is dying. Anyone who isn't troubled by that has no conscience."

McCrae cocked his head. Hamish's bloodshot eyes were dull with dark circles beneath them.

"Don't look at me like that. You remind me of the crow that stands outside my bedroom."

"Yer not sleeping."

"I have not long buried my uncle and taken in his rebellious daughter. When you are wed to her, you'll not sleep either."

"Are you seeing ghosts?"

Hamish picked up Bran's reins. "Yer not locking me away with lunatics."

"I'm worried about you. Yer the only family Katrein has."

"There's nothing wrong with me that ale won't cure." Hamish clicked his tongue and the cart trundled down Fleshmarket Close opposite.

THE MALIGNANT DEAD

McCrae returned to his loft to collect the last of his herbs. If the council didn't pay him soon, he would have to steal them. He opened the door and saw a box on his bed. He picked up the note attached to the lid.

Since the council first refused to pay you, I have been buying herbs from the market. I do not believe you will see that wage they promised. Consider these herbs an early wedding present.

J

P.S. Before the plague rendered me useless, I took it upon myself to dress as a peasant and spy on that wretch, Andrews. He is following you. I have included a list of his haunts. Beware.

McCrae opened the box. Bunches of herbs, chunks of brimstone, pouches of tobacco and phials of potions greeted him. Shaking his head, he fetched a bag and emptied the box into it. He trotted down the stairs.

McCrae stopped at Clyde's lodgings on Warden's Close off Grassmarket. Like most of the closes in Edinburgh, the buildings towered above him, some reaching fifteen stories high. The buildings were pressed close together because the Flodden Wall meant the only way they could cope with the growing population was to build up. The Flodden Wall had taken fifty-three years to build, to keep the English out. It had not kept the English out; it kept the Scottish in.

The watchman let him in.

"Clyde? Are you well?"

Clyde lay on the bed, blood trickling from the corner of his mouth and dripping onto his straw-filled pillow. His rigid fingers clutched his moth-eaten blankets and an empty phial.

McCrae dropped onto the edge of the bed, his head in his hands. His bag fell to the floor, bundles of herbs escaping. His cures were as helpful as Petrie's rabbit foot. His heart thumped in the silence, reminding him he was one of the few still alive. Sick dread consumed him. His jaw clenched, hot tears pricking his eyes.

"I'm sorry. I thought I could cure you. I cannot cure anyone. I might as well be using unicorn horn for all the good I've done. Folk are right – I should go back to Dad's market stall and sell his linen to shroud the dead."

McCrae picked up Clyde and carried him to the door. The watchman opened it as a cart passed on Grassmarket.

"Bring out yer dead!"

A door opened across the street and a woman carried her bairn to the cart. Her red eyes betrayed her misery as she laid the lad amongst the dead.

"Why can you not save them?" She struck McCrae's back. He stumbled, nearly dropping Clyde. "My wee laddie is *dead*! Is God punishing me because I conceived him out of wedlock?"

McCrae lay Clyde beside the lad, on top of an old man with blackened, rotting skin. "This has not come from God."

"Pastor Matthews says we're being punished for our sins and prayer will keep the plague away. Did I not pray enough?"

"If God was punishing us, he would infect the wicked, not the innocent. Blame God if it makes you feel better, but prayers won't save you." Nothing would. He could not give her hope, only nightmares.

"We will all die." She ran into her tenement, sobbing.

McCrae returned to Clyde's tenement and collected his bag and spilled herbs. He closed the door and handed the watchman a pouch of tobacco. "Summon the clengers."

"Is she right?" The watchman nodded towards Grassmarket. "Are we all going to die?"

"We're not dead yet."

McCrae emerged on Grassmarket. He glanced up to see Fergusson's pet, Andrews, lurking in the shadows. When he looked again, Andrews had gone.

Chapter 12

Rain hammered the window of James's room then slithered down the glass in defeat; tears of the damned streaking the pane with their misery.

James lay in bed writing notes. "I hate rain. It disturbs the loch and brings the stench to the surface."

"The loch always smells." McCrae moved away from the window to the table. He didn't like the way the dead plant watched him.

"Perhaps the council created the plague to rid the city of scoundrels." James shivered and pulled the blankets tighter around his skeletal frame. "The wealthy will return when the peasants have moved to their new home in Gray-friar."

"I could believe that." McCrae picked up a mandrake root. It looked like a person. "The council have survived it after all. The ones who stayed. Maybe they created their own elixir."

"I say we put forth our evidence and have them hanged for murder."

"What evidence?"

"The rich fled and the poor died."

"Yer rich and you have the plague."

"They infected me because they knew I would discover their nefarious plot, but they did not foresee my potions allowing me to live long enough to expose their treachery."

"Is it the plague or yer potions making you insane?"

"How do we know insanity is not the purest form of sanity?" James tapped his quill against his page. "I hid my intelligence beneath a disguise of insanity to expose the council's devious ways without suspicion. Like Hamlet. There is method in my madness."

"Hamlet killed three people then died from poisoning."

"Horatio lived to spread the word of Hamlet's genius." James winked then coughed, his gasps raspy. McCrae rushed to him but James waved him away. "Perhaps the council infected me because I am friends with you. My father always said you would be my ruin." He read his notes. "Add two drops of the red liquid to the poppy seeds then crush them and sprinkle that white powder in."

"Are you making this up?" McCrae tapped two drops of red liquid from a tube onto the tiny black poppy seeds and ground the seeds. He looked away from the ruby roses decorating James's skin. He was certain beneath the herbs hanging from the bed he could smell James's skin rotting.

"I have worked everything out to the last drop. Man of science, remember?"

"Have you tested this on another plant? Will Edinburgh be overrun with dead plants marching through the streets, eating anyone who crosses their path? I'm not trained to cure that. Though I'm not trained to cure the plague either."

"Don't be daft, Alex. Plants cannot walk." James studied him. "You should be wearing your bird costume. You're amongst the diseased."

"And deny you my handsome face?"

"Have I not suffered enough?"

McCrae laughed and added the white powder from another pot and mixed it with the seeds.

"Has work started on my James Lowther Institute?"

"You have not cured the plague."

"I have created a brilliant potion that regenerates hair growth." James removed his hat. His thinning hair was thick again.

"They don't name institutes after people who cure hair loss and poison themselves."

"Your lack of faith is heart-breaking, Alex."

"You would still have yer hair had you not ingested arsenic." McCrae emptied the powder into a crucible.

"It is too late for regrets. Pour that clear liquid in until the crucible is half full and mix it until the powder has dissolved."

McCrae obeyed, stirring the powder and watching the grains swirl. "Katrein drank yer potion."

"Why on earth did you give it to her? That was asking for trouble."

"She took it from my pocket when she kissed me."

"That old trick." James chuckled. "How much did she drink?"

"The whole phial."

James rested his quill against his page, his breathing shallow. "Has she grown hair all over her body? Grown taller? Shrunk? Has she started singing at inappropriate times and shedding her clothing?"

McCrae laughed. "No."

"That's a shame." James dipped his quill into his inkpot. The quill quivered. He steadied it with his other hand. Ink dripped onto his page. "If anything it will merely make her sick for a day or two. I wonder..." he tapped his chin. "Maybe I could create a love potion that will enable me to steal her from you. As my oldest friend and with me being a dying man, you will bear no grudges."

"I could slip poison into yer love potion and pretend a witch cursed you for using black magic."

"You're a cruel man, Alex McCrae, and I *will* live to see you burned for witchcraft."

McCrae laughed again. "Is this why I'm mixing the potion? So you can record this as evidence?"

"Why would a beautiful lady like Katrein and a handsome rogue such as myself, have fallen for your charms without enchantment? If you will not allow me to wed your betrothed, perhaps you will allow me to wed your daughter. She would be a pleasing combination of both of you."

"There would be nobody else I would wish for my daughter to marry. Except for yer son."

"And they shall produce our heir."

"At least theirs would not hide in St Giles and feast on folk."

James narrowed his eyes. "It may. It will still have your blood."

McCrae smiled and brought the crucible of blood red liquid over. "What will this do?"

"Either rid my pestilent body of this disease or cause me to grow breasts and you will fall madly in love with me. I'm sure you have already and had I been born a woman, we would have married years ago. But alas I was cursed with a man's body and denied your manly affections."

"Had *I* been born a lass—"

"You would have been ugly."

James drank half the potion then relinquished the crucible to McCrae and pulled his blankets higher.

McCrae sniffed the liquid. "It smells better than most of them." He drank it then swayed, nearly dropping the crucible. He shuffled to the table and put the crucible down. It smashed on the floor. "Shit." He grabbed the table to stop himself joining the crucible.

"Maybe I used too many seeds. Either that or God is spinning this building at a frightening speed." James shut his eyes. "My God, I have created something more powerful than ale. Alert the inn! We shall be rich!"

"You *are* rich."

"You're not."

"We're supposed to be curing the plague, not getting drunk."

"I thought we were making history. Alex, I have cured pain! I could leap from this bed and dance down the street."

"I hope not. You dance like a drunk."

"I dance like an angel."

McCrae held his hands out as he walked to James's bed and slumped onto it. "Tell yer bed to stay still." The blankets muffled his voice.

"Bed, stay still. You are making us dizzy."

"I have to...cut open...someone." McCrae pushed himself to his feet. "The deacon! I have to dissect the deacon."

"I don't think he would like that."

McCrae stumbled towards the door and hit the floor with a thud.

James laughed so hard, a coughing fit attacked him. "What are you doing down there?"

McCrae rolled onto his side. "I was cutting open the deacon." He laughed then rolled onto his back. The ceiling spun. He groaned. "I think I'm dying."

"Send the devil my regards."

"Send them yerself."

"I cannot. I will live forever. To immortality!" James coughed.

McCrae raised an imaginary toast. His arm flopped onto his chest as he laughed. The shrivelled plant looked six feet high, with razor leaves and vicious teeth. "Don't eat me."

"I can barely keep these potions down, I will never manage you."

McCrae flipped onto his front and forced himself to his knees. His eyes fought to focus. Thick fog seeped into his head and crept along the passages in his mind.

"I cannot treat patients like this. I will go to lance their buboes and take out their eyes." McCrae struggled to his feet and staggered back to the bed. He collapsed face down onto it. He twisted onto his back and shuffled up the bed until he rested against the headboard. Loud ticking echoed around the room. The plant turned to look at him.

McCrae rubbed his temples. "Yer watch is loud."

"It's that damn beetle. It haunts me in the darkest hours."

McCrae closed his eyes until the room stopped spinning. James's head rested on his shoulder. He opened his eyes and glanced at James. Blood droplets stained his hands and his page.

"Andrews was in Grassmarket yesterday. Today I saw him near the Cowgate gorge."

"You should have pushed him in. I warned you about the council."

"They offered the wage; I didn't demand it."

James patted McCrae's hand. "What you do not understand about the rich and powerful is that they are never rich or powerful enough. The council will never pay you."

"Then why offer that amount?"

"To tempt you into taking the position. How long was Petrie the plague doctor?"

"A week."

"How long have you been the plague doctor?"

"Nearly six weeks."

"You were supposed to die so they would not have to pay you."

"They want me to die?"

"You should quit."

"Not now we're curing folk. The council need me."

James shrugged. "Not as much as they need money. Andrews gets rid of people who cause Fergusson problems. Soon, *you* will be the problem."

James coughed. He tried taking a breath, but the cough consumed him. McCrae pulled a rag from his pocket and wiped the blood trickling down James's chin. Through James's open shirt, blackened skin taunted him.

Ticking echoed through the room, chilling McCrae's blood.

"Pass me that..." James wheezed and pointed. His hand trembled. "The blue-green one."

McCrae fetched the phial and sat back on the bed. "Will it turn you into a snake? Make you breathe fire?"

"Sadly not." James drank the entire phial.

"What is it?"

"Poison. And plant food."

Burning tears blurred McCrae's vision. "No," he whispered. He slapped the phial out of James's hand. It slid along the floor, spinning. "Spit it out!"

Nausea flooded him, dread festering in his gut. A noose of fear strangled his chest and stomach. He forced open James's mouth and pushed his fingers down his throat. James gagged and fought him off. McCrae leapt off the bed and ran to the worktable. He ransacked the flasks, knocking potions over.

"Which one induces vomiting?"

"I don't wish to vomit. Don't worry, Alex. That potion you made killed my pain."

"It has not killed mine! I will *not* let you die!" He flung open James's trunk, rummaging through his clothes. "Where is yer knife? I will perform bloodletting until the poison has left yer body."

"I have made copious notes so you can continue my work."

"I don't *want* to continue yer work. I want *you* to continue it! I'm not an apothecary, I'm a linen seller." McCrae tugged open a drawer, searching through it. "Where is yer bloody knife?"

"You cannot save everyone, Alex."

"I don't *want* to save *everyone*. I want to save *you*!" McCrae darted back to the table and picked up various phials, checking their labels. "Where's the antidote?"

"I didn't make one. If my father tries to have me buried in London, punch him. I want a mausoleum so big there won't be room for anyone else in Gray-friar. Gregor will have to dig the pits in the streets. I want a monument so tall you can see it from every tenement, corner and shadow of Edinburgh. Every time King Charles looks out from the castle, he will be consumed with rage and envy because he'll think I must have been a great man to deserve such a monument."

"You don't want much."

"I'm a modest man."

"Self-murder is a sin. You know what they will do to you!"

"I will be dead. I care not what they do to me."

"*I* care!" McCrae swiped his burning eyes. "I don't wish to see you dragged through the streets, or hung by yer ankles then buried on the highway. I could not bear that. You will be ripped apart in Hell for eternity."

"If thoughts count as sin, I am bound for Hell anyway. I might as well make my stay worthwhile. Thomas More said that a person afflicted with disease can 'free himself from this bitter life…since by death he will put an end not to enjoyment but to torture…it will be a pious and holy action'. I shall be ruling Heaven in a fortnight."

"*Please*, James. A life without you is no life at all."

"Come here."

McCrae trudged back to the bed and lay beside James, hugging him to his chest. James rested his arms around McCrae's side.

"You cannot suffocate me, you don't have breasts." James's voice was muffled.

McCrae laughed, tears sliding down his cheeks and dripping onto James's head.

"If I cannot save you, the least I can do is not let you die alone. We shall see if yer potion works."

McCrae stroked James's hair, his body shaking as he fought to repress his tears. His chest ached, his throat feeling as though burning brimstone was lodged in it. He kissed James's forehead. After each laboured breath James took, sick anticipation consumed McCrae as he waited to see if he would take another, dreading the moment he didn't.

"To immortality!"

James's arm slipped down McCrae's side.

Chapter 13

McCrae squeezed James against his chest in the vain hope his heart could make James's beat again. Scalding tears crawled down his face, his eyes and throat burning. He gasped, his chest feeling as though his heart was breaking. The pain spreading through his body, through his mind, was worse than poison. It consumed him, tortured him, broke him, but he would not die from its agony so was forced to suffer it without reprieve.

Maybe death was not the cruellest fate a person could suffer.

The ticking stopped.

He laid James down and rose from the bed. Snatching up the poison phial, he hurled it against the wall. The fragments fell like crystal tears, but it did nothing to ease the pain. He gathered the pieces, touching them to his tongue. He flung James's notebook at the alembics and flasks. Some toppled, others fractured on the floor. He knocked flasks off with his arm, throwing others against the wall or floor. He wanted to tear out his heart and smash it against the wall until he could no longer feel the wound ripping it in half.

"All his potions and I could not save *one life*!"

McCrae sank to the floor, kneeling amongst the shattered glass and spilled liquid as he sobbed. He grabbed an empty bowl and vomited into it, his stomach cramping.

He wiped his mouth, his hand trembling. James's hand hung off the bed, his fingers stained scarlet. McCrae watched for any signs of life.

There were none.

He stood and picked up the notebook. A loose page fell out. He unfolded it.

My Dearest Alex,

We knew I would not survive this. Do not blame yourself. The Fates decide the length of our mortal coils and I have reached the end of mine. I merely denied them the pleasure of cutting the thread. You know I always liked having my own way.

Under my bed is a box of coins. It is not what the council owes you but it should help. If you do not take it, I will haunt you.

If I am not resurrected, I will see you in the next life. If Heaven exists, I am already its new ruler. It is better to be king of the dead than servant of the living.

The rightful King James VII of Scotland. Doctor, friend, hero.

McCrae smiled, his tears falling faster. The ink on the page was still wet. Smudged ink droplets and blood spray stained the paper. A tear splashed the page, causing the J to bleed.

McCrae sat on the bed and cradled James against his chest until his tears ran dry. James's head flopped backwards onto McCrae's shoulder.

"What do I tell yer father? I could not save you so you took yer own life? He will disown you." McCrae stroked James's hair and stared at the dead plant. "I could say nothing, but he will fetch you to London to be buried in yer family's mausoleum. Forgive my selfishness, but I want you here. Edinburgh without you is not my home." He touched James's lips, but no breath escaped. "I could say everyone must be buried immediately, whether they die by the plague or other means. He would have to leave you here. But self-murder is a sin. Nobody is without sin, yet their bodies are not dragged through the streets and buried on the highway. Why should you suffer that fate? You have harmed nobody but yerself." He wrapped his arms around James's chest. "I know what I *must* do, according to God's will, yet…my heart says differently."

McCrae closed his aching eyes. When he opened them, the sky had darkened as though day had had her throat cut and her black blood spilled across the clouds.

"James?" He tapped James's cool cheek.

McCrae slipped out from behind James and lowered him to the pillow. He knelt by the bed and pulled a box from underneath it. Opening it, he stared at the coins sitting inside. Taking a handful, he forced himself to his feet and donned his cloak and mask. His reflection taunted him in the mirror, as though it watched him from the land of the dead, surrounded by all the folk he had failed to save. Freeing a half-empty phial from his pocket, he flung it, fracturing the glass. Only his broken reflection remained.

He walked out. The rattling of the death carts chilled his blood. Shaking, blackened fingers pushed a fresh white rag through a window. McCrae walked past, hoping he didn't encounter anyone he knew. He would not be able to speak. He felt like a stranger in his own body. He walked until he reached the carpenter's tenement. No cross burdened the door. He banged on it until a candle appeared behind the door. The carpenter, Patrick, opened it, wearing his nightshirt.

Patrick's eyes widened. "We're not infected! Go away!"

McCrae pushed down his hood and tugged the mask off. "I need a coffin."

"Come back at a decent hour. The dead will not rise and walk away."

McCrae gripped the doorframe and pushed the coins into Patrick's hand. "I need a coffin *now*."

"It will be ready by dawn."

"Can you not work quicker?"

"You've dragged me out of bed, demanded a coffin and now you want it quickly? I should send you away. I cannot work faster than that."

McCrae walked to Gray-friar. He took a spade from beside the newest pit to a secluded spot in the corner of the kirkyard closest to the castle. He stabbed the spade into the grass, stamped on it then tossed the grass aside. Rage drove him on after his arms tired. When he had dug three feet deep, he sat on the edge of the grave. His mask watched from the headstone of the neighbouring grave. The night air cooled the sweat on his body. Moaning roamed the kirkyard. He wasn't sure if it was the cry of the relentless wind or the restless dead.

By the time McCrae had finished, dawn's grey fingers prised through the night's dark cloak to peek at the horrors lurking below. He returned to Patrick's, feeling drained of everything except exhaustion and sorrow.

Patrick opened the door. "I have finished."

"Thank you."

McCrae trailed him to where the coffin waited on a table. Tears pricked his eyes at the thought of James lying in there, buried beneath the ground for eternity. The coffin made it real.

James was never coming back.

McCrae paid Patrick extra for his trouble. Slipping into his cloak and mask, he asked Patrick to place the coffin on his back then carried it towards James's house.

"Another new role, Doctor Death? Driving death carts, making coffins – soon you will be running the death trade single-handedly."

McCrae turned. Bran whinnied and threw up his head, his eyes wide.

"Ssh, it's McCrae. He's scarier without the mask, laddie." Hamish leaned forwards and patted Bran's rump. "Put that in the back."

Hamish joined him at the back of the cart and helped slide the coffin in. Hamish hopped back into the cart and slapped the seat. McCrae climbed up.

"Where to, Doctor Death?"

"James's." McCrae looked away.

"I'm sorry, laddie." Hamish squeezed his shoulder then flicked his reins and guided Bran towards Niddry Wynd.

McCrae swayed with the cart as they passed white rags and red crosses. There was barely a tenement that had escaped the plague, especially in the narrow wynds and closes. He could not cure it. All he could do was make folk's homes smell better then dump folk on the cart when his methods failed yet again. His failure as a doctor was displayed from every tenement, each white rag proving folk right that his place was at the market stall, not in the Craft.

Hamish stopped outside the tenement and helped McCrae unload the coffin. They carried it up to James's room and laid it on the floor.

"I'll fetch Katrein." Hamish's footsteps clumped down the stairs.

McCrae stared at James's body. "I cannot believe I'll never see you again. Never hear yer voice. Never laugh at yer ideas. How can I live without you? I cannot put you in that box in the ground. I cannot say—" he swallowed a sob, "—goodbye."

He fetched James's pillow and laid it in the coffin then he found his best clothes. McCrae could not understand why folk called death the eternal sleep. James didn't look like he was sleeping. McCrae resisted the grief threatening to consume him and dressed James. James's head flopped to the side. McCrae tried taking deep breaths to quell the pain burning a hole in his chest, but choked. He picked James up and placed him in the coffin.

Wiping his eyes, he grabbed an alembic and a phial of potion, arranged them beside James, then sat on a chair.

"You raised that plant from death. You probably drank that potion to frighten me when the time came to bury you."

James's pale, blotchy skin showed no sign of life. Just death.

"Come on James. Prove what a genius you are."

James didn't move.

"I'm so sorry!" Katrein burst into the room and flung her arms around McCrae. He could not bring himself to raise his arms and return the affection. Katrein turned, saw James and crumpled to the floor, covering her mouth with her hand. "I didn't believe Hamish, but it's true. Would you like me to sit with you during the wake?"

"I have held the wake."

"And he has not stirred?"

"He made a potion to bring the dead to life. He's coming back."

"You cannot come back from death, Alex. That's fanciful thinking. The mind plays tricks in grief."

McCrae gestured to the plant. "I *saw* it rise from death."

"It's dead."

"It drinks."

"It's still dead." Katrein rose and hugged McCrae's head to her chest, leaning down to kiss his hair. "James was full of fantasy. He thought he could fly, remember?" She crouched and stroked the splint. She placed James's cane in the coffin then kissed his forehead. "Goodnight James."

"He will wake. He promised me."

"He won't."

"I will not bury him until I'm certain! His potions have probably induced a coma. I cannot bear the thought of him waking in the coffin, unable to escape."

"We could tie string around his finger and tie the other end to a bell on the graveside. Once he moves his hand, the bell will ring, Gregor will hear it and we can save him."

McCrae nodded.

Katrein found string in a drawer. She tied one end around James's finger then pushed it through a breathing hole in the coffin. "We need a bell."

Moments later, a bell tinkled. McCrae closed his eyes as Hamish handed it to Katrein. The bell reminded him of death carts, the plague, and his dead friend.

Katrein cut the string and tied the other end to the bell.

Hamish picked up the coffin lid, his eyes wet. "Yer burying him in his clothes? Don't you want to keep them or sell them?"

"When he wakes, he will be upset to find he is naked. He cannot walk the streets in a shroud."

McCrae dropped to his knees beside the coffin. He grabbed James's hand, his tears splashing his friend's face. He leaned forwards, kissing his head.

"I will cure this plague and kill whoever started it. Goodbye James. I'll make sure yer memory lives forever, even if you don't."

Hamish lowered the lid.

"Don't nail it shut. It must be easy for him to escape."

"Men don't come back from the dead."

"Then what is it you see?" McCrae said through clenched teeth.

"Ghosts. Not the living dead."

"I don't see how one is possible but not the other."

"Because the other would be too nightmarish to witness. A spirit can live forever. A body cannot."

Hamish draped a blanket over the cracked mirror.

McCrae wiped his eyes. "What are you doing?"

"It will stop his spirit from returning and being trapped in the glass."

Hamish and McCrae carried the coffin down the stairs to the cart. An empty string dangled where the bell used to hang. Katrein and Hamish rode up front while McCrae sat in the back.

"That's where the dead ride," Hamish warned.

"Soon we will all be among the dead. I might as well enjoy it while I am alive."

Hamish flicked the reins and Bran walked through the streets, the bell tolling for another death in the city of ghosts.

Chapter 14

Rain splattered the wooden cross marking the grave then sank into the churned earth, as though the clouds shed the tears McCrae could not. He hoped James wasn't getting wet. He had never been fond of the rain. Hamish's bell hung from the cross's horizontal bar. A cover protected the bell to prevent it ringing in the wind. Rain pattered McCrae's hooded cloak. He imagined he could hear the bell ringing as loudly as the bell in the Tolbooth signalling the opening of the market.

"He's not coming back." Katrein wrapped one arm around his back while the other held her skirt above the wet ground. "How many nights will you stand at his grave? Soon you'll be sleeping in there with him."

McCrae closed his eyes, raindrops streaking the eyes of the mask.

"You haven't spoken since we buried him. I hate seeing you so...broken. My heart bleeds when I look at you."

McCrae walked away, averting his gaze from the large mound of earth. It was as though the kirkyard's heart had been ripped out, leaving a crusted wound. Katrein scuttled after him, tripping over a headstone and nearly landing on another. She cursed, wiping her muddy hands on her skirt.

"How do you do it?" he asked.

"Fall on my face? It's easy when you wear skirts." Katrein linked her arm through his. "I wish I could wear breeches."

"How do you go on living when someone you love has died? You buried yer parents, yet you are not wallowing in yer grief."

"You and Hamish are my reasons to keep living. I wallow in my grief in the wee hours when Hamish is being haunted by his nightmares and yers are keeping you awake. I wear a mask, like you. Mine mirrors my real face."

"Do you think of joining them in death?"

She stared at him. "Don't talk of such things! If you self-destruct, I will dig you up and murder you myself! Don't you *dare* leave me alone in this world."

"You have Hamish."

"I won't have *you*."

"If God does not wish for folk to murder themselves, he should not make their lives unbearable. If someone is dying, why should they not choose how they die? I don't see why folks' corpses are punished for this."

"Yer not dying."

"Something inside me has died. I would give my soul to the devil for one more day with James."

"If Pastor Matthews hears you speak of such Godless acts, he will have you burned at the stake!"

They left the kirkyard and walked down Candlemaker Row towards Grassmarket.

"What if forcing people to live until the Fates sever their mortal coil is the real selfish act? Isn't it kinder to end their suffering?"

"Alex! Yer talking of murder."

"Can it be murder if it is done with kindness?"

"It's God's will when someone dies."

"The judge decides when someone dies. Is that not murder? You asked me to help you should you catch the plague."

"Alex, yer grieving, so I forgive yer insane ramblings. But I cannot take you seriously when you talk of murder whilst dressed as a bird."

McCrae gave a short laugh. "Promise me you'll never die."

"I cannot. But I can promise to kill you before I die so we can haunt Hamish together. The poor man would never sleep again!"

"Why isn't James a ghost?"

"He didn't die violently and he has no wrongs to right or any unfinished business."

"He didn't cure death. That's a good reason to stay."

"Death *cannot* be cured."

They walked in silence until they reached High Street. A shadow flitted behind the Luckenbooths. This row of tenements joined to the Tolbooth narrowed the street to fourteen feet and got its name from the locked booths or shops on the ground floor. McCrae raised his lantern. Perhaps he would not have to seek Death. Perhaps Death had found him.

Motioning for Katrein to stay, he relinquished his lantern to her and crept around the Luckenbooths, slipping his lance from his pocket. Without his lantern, the streets were darker than a grave. He darted into Auld Kirk Style, or Stinking Style, the passage between the Luckenbooths and St Giles, and seized a man by the coat as he tried to hide in one of the open fronted krames that sold toys. Katrein trotted over with the lantern.

"Andrews, isn't it? Fergusson's pet."

Andrews wriggled. "Unhand me! Or I'll cut yer throat."

"Are the council paying you to follow me?"

"I don't know what yer talking about."

McCrae punched him. Andrews's head snapped backwards, blood trickling from his nose. "Has yer memory improved?" He hit him again, splitting Andrews's lip. "Why are you following me?"

"I'm not!"

McCrae released Andrews's coat and thumped him to the ground. That felt better than smashing James's flasks and alembics. For the first time since James died, he didn't feel completely dead. He raised his foot.

"Alex!" Katrein chastised. "Dead men cannot speak."

Andrews's eyes widened. "Please don't kill me!"

"I saw you talking to Fergusson weeks ago in the market and now wherever I am, there you are too."

Andrews struggled up and swung at McCrae. The blow glanced off his beak. "I'm making sure yer keeping to the terms of yer role."

"I am. The council is not."

"You'll regret this."

Andrews threw another punch. McCrae ducked and struck Andrews's chin, sending him sprawling. He placed his boot on Andrews's chest, leaned down and pressed his lance beneath Andrews's eye.

"Tell the council if they don't pay me, I will tell the town crier and anyone who will listen that they are liars and thieves. The next time I see you, I will put you on the death cart. I don't care if yer still breathing. When yer lying in the pit, surrounded by the putrid corpses of the folk I failed to save, you'll realise death is not the worst thing that can befall someone."

***

A knock rattled the door, like an awakening corpse banging on his coffin lid to be set free to feast on the unwary. Fergusson put down his book and rose from his armchair beside the hearth. He opened the door. The lantern beside his door bathed Andrews's bloodied face in a fiery glow, as though he had crawled from Hell to prowl Edinburgh.

Fergusson glared. "I told you never to darken my door."

"Unless you want to discuss matters on yer doorstep in front of yer neighbours, let me in."

Fergusson glowered but stepped aside. He scanned Covenant Close before closing the door. At least the plague had reduced the number of people who would betray him. Threats could be stopped by locking the accuser in their home and painting a red cross on their door.

"I know the location of every possession, so if you steal something, I will see you hanged."

"If you hang me, my last words would be a confession. You'll swing beside me. You have *far* more to lose than I do."

Fergusson looked Andrews up and down disdainfully. "What the devil happened to you?"

"McCrae caught me spying on him. He said if you don't pay him, he'll tell the town crier that the council are liars and thieves. Then he threatened to kill me."

Fergusson's jaw clenched. "Why has that insufferable ruffian not caught the plague yet? I suspect he made a deal with the devil."

"Maybe his terrifying costume works."

"Make it *stop* working. I have worked hard on the council and I will not be thrown in the Tolbooth to hang like some wretched criminal because of a greedy market trader's son who does not know his place!"

"Threats against him will not frighten him. Threats against those he loves will. Should someone have a word with Miss Reid, it will make him listen."

Fergusson paced the carpet. Without a plague doctor, the city would die. Without the council, it would never live again. He stared at the fire, as though he could find the answers in the writhing flames.

"Very well. Nobody must hear of this. Not Douglas and Kilbride, not your ruffian friends and certainly not any whores from the inn. A woman can coax any secret from a man once she has him by the cock."

"I won't say anything."

Fergusson narrowed his eyes. He trusted Andrews as much as he trusted a starving man in a bakery. He hoped Andrews caught the plague and died before he told a soul. Maybe McCrae would silence Andrews for him. Then he could throw McCrae in the Tolbooth. Fergusson would not hang like a thief. People would believe the word of a councillor over a rogue. Wealth bought far more than nice houses and fine possessions.

Fergusson faced Andrews. "If threatening Miss Reid is the only way to silence McCrae then so be it. But do not under any circumstances, kill her. There is nothing more dangerous than a man who has lost everything."

Chapter 15

Katrein unravelled the bandage from the farmer's foot and examined his severed toes. "It's healing nicely. But you must keep it clean or it will get infected." She fetched a bowl of water then returned to his bedside and cleaned the wounds. "You don't want me returning with an axe and leaving with yer foot like beef from the market."

"I work in the mud, lass. I cannot keep my hat clean, let alone my foot."

Katrein smiled and wrapped his foot in cloth then replaced the bandage. "Next time, put yer spade into the ground, not yer foot."

"I'll try." He winced. "Is it true you are to wed the plague doctor? The one in the scary mask?"

"He's not so scary without the mask, thankfully, or I would have to ask him to keep it on."

He shivered. "I would not want to see him when I'm on my death bed. If Death was a person, he'd dress like that."

She laughed. "That must be why they call him Doctor Death. I'll return tomorrow."

"You cannot walk these streets alone, lass! When my lad returns from the inn, he will see you safely home."

"I don't wish to trouble him. I will likely see my cousin and his cart. I will ride with him."

"I will walk you."

"Not with yer foot like that. Don't worry, I can look after myself."

She let herself out and hastened towards her last patient's house. Night embraced the streets, hiding the devils beneath its cloak. She was looking forwards to sitting by the fire with Hamish and listening to his tales about who he had on his cart. Laughter echoed from one of the closes. It had been a while since she had heard laughter instead of tears and cries of anguish. Happiness was no longer an emotion Edinburgh possessed.

"Excuse me?"

She jumped and reeled around, raising her lantern. Unease crawled over her flesh. She stepped backwards and glanced around the deserted street. Over the cries of the dying, no-one would hear her screams.

A man stepped forwards. "Are you McCrae's betrothed?"

"Aye," she drew out the word. "He's meeting me now," she lied. "Do you wish to speak to him?" She took another step back, gripping her lantern.

"I want you to deliver a message."

He grabbed her and dragged her down an alley. She shrieked before he covered her mouth with his hand. She wriggled and kicked, but he held her firm. He threw her to the ground then straddled her, his hand over her mouth. Her heart raced. She could not breathe. His hand stank of ale, leather and sweat. His weight hurt her legs. She thought she had experienced fear before. She was wrong.

"Tell McCrae to keep his mouth shut or I will cut out his tongue."

She bit his hand. He yelled and slapped her across the face. Her lip stung and she tasted blood.

"Get off me or I'll rip out yer tongue and feed it to the crows." She spat her blood and his foul taste at him.

"You were spirited last time. This time I *will* tame you."

Kneeing him in the groin would not save her now. She clawed his face, leaving scarlet slashes.

"You vicious bitch!" He slapped her again. "You will learn respect."

Her cheek smarted. "You don't deserve respect."

He pinned her by the throat with one arm while his other hand raised her skirts. She gasped, her vision turning blue. If she passed out, she was done for. She snatched her lantern and struck him across the head. He hissed and punched her in the face again. Her cheekbone throbbed. She crossed her ankles, squeezing her thighs together as he tried forcing her legs apart. Terror engulfed her. This could not be happening.

"Spread yer legs like the whore you are."

Tears drowned her eyes. The only person she would give herself to was Alex. She would rather die than let this scoundrel take her by force. He leaned down to wriggle his hand between her thighs, pinching her skin. She sank her teeth into his jaw. He yelled and punched her, but she refused to release him. If she did, a worse fate awaited her.

"Get off her!"

Hamish grabbed her attacker around the throat and hurled him to the floor. He kicked him in the ribs.

"Kat!"

He lowered Katrein's skirts then helped her up and hugged her. Katrein opened her lantern and grabbed the candle. She dropped to her knees and held it against the man's groin while he screamed, his breeches aflame with burning pig fat.

"So you can never hurt another lass!"

The man slapped the flames until they died.

Hamish pulled her up. "Run."

Hamish stumbled as the man hit him on the back of his head. He whirled around and flattened the man with one punch.

"You think attacking lasses makes you a man?" Hamish asked. "It makes you scum."

The man rose, clutching his loins with his blistered hands. Hamish kicked him in the face.

"Kat, go."

She wiped her eyes, marched towards the fallen man and stamped on his throat. "This time, *I* will tame *you*."

He gurgled and writhed. "He made me."

"Who?" She pressed harder. "Tell me or I will crush yer throat like a trampled weed."

"Andrews."

Dread crawled through her body and she removed her foot.

He leapt to his feet and shoved her into the wall. She groaned as she hit her head.

"You don't learn fast," Hamish said.

The man fled.

Hamish whistled. Bran blocked the alley with his cart. Hamish chuckled as he walked to the man and punched him in the face. The ruffian's head cracked against the wall and he crumpled to the floor. Hamish picked him up then tossed him into the cart. He whistled again and Bran pulled the cart past the alley.

Hamish returned to Katrein and parted her hair. He kissed her wound then walked to the cart. "You coming?"

"Where?"

"Gray-friar. I have passengers to deliver to their new home."

Katrein wiped her eyes, trailed him to the cart and climbed in, tugging her cloak around her. She shook as the horror revisited her.

Hamish flicked the reins and Bran walked on. "You would not believe who I had in my cart."

She fought the tears, but they kept falling. "Who?"

"One of King Charles's soldiers. He sat with me and told me secrets about the king that would make you faint."

"I have never fainted."

"Did you know he makes furniture out of his enemies' bones? And his hair is made from the hair of his mistresses?"

She forced herself to smile. "It isn't!"

"And King Charles likes to wear dresses and dance with handsome suitors."

She chuckled. "They will hang you for treason."

"Only if you tell them."

They rode into Gray-friar and Hamish stopped his cart on the edge of the pit. Gregor was nowhere to be seen.

The bodies slipped into the pit.

"Is he dead?" Katrein pointed to her attacker as he tumbled out with the corpses. She curled her trembling hand into a fist.

Hamish placed his arm around Katrein's shoulders. "Hope not." A groan rumbled from the pit. Katrein glanced at Hamish. "Men who rape lasses deserve to die a horrible death. I wish I had a knife so I could cut his cock off and feed it to him. What if I had not come along? What if Andrews had? This is why McCrae and I don't like you walking alone. Many men see lasses for one thing only."

"Andrews works for Councillor Fergusson. He's been threatening Alex."

"If this is the council's doing, we cannot turn this man over. The pit is the best place for him. Even if they hanged him, he would end up here. We're saving them money. They should reward us." He rubbed Katrein's arm. "I'll take you home."

She shook her head. "I won't feel safe until I know that man is dead. Every footstep I hear, every shadow behind me, every male voice I'll think it's him."

"He won't scare you again." Hamish fetched a spade and tossed mud over the pit. Some of the bodies shifted as the man awoke. Through the entangled limbs, his frightened eyes watched them.

"Help me!"

"I will help you to die." Hamish smiled. "Tell the devil Hamish Reid sent you."

He threw earth over the man's eyes, working swiftly until that section of the pit was covered.

"What are you doing?" Gregor asked. His gait was unsteady and his breath smelled of scotch.

"Don't want the dead crawling out. Edinburgh has enough corpses without them walking the streets."

"I heard something."

"Another sinner making a deal with the devil. You've been around the dead too long, Gregor. Yer hearing ghosts. The scotch is playing tricks on you." Hamish linked his arm through Katrein's and steered her towards Bran. Once they left Gray-friar, Katrein burst into tears. Hamish stopped the cart and held her.

"If you had not come…"

"You would have chewed off his face. I was rescuing him, not you."

"Nobody would marry a lass who's been spoiled."

Hamish stroked Katrein's hair. "McCrae loves you and he would marry you even if that monster had raped you. But you fought him off. My brave lass." He kissed her head. "Now he can rot amongst the plague-riddled. With any luck his cock will still be burning in Hell." He chuckled. "I have never heard a man scream like that."

"If I see Andrews, I will ram my foot so far up his bunghole he will taste toes for weeks."

Hamish tucked her hair behind her ear. "Yer mam and dad would be proud of how strong you are."

"I don't feel strong."

He squeezed her knee. "If you won't go home, you will ride with me for the night."

Katrein wiped her eyes. "I have one more patient."

"I'll stand outside looking mean. Maybe I should borrow McCrae's mask to frighten lowlifes away."

"You don't need his mask, yer face will do the task just as well."

Hamish laughed and poked her in the ribs. He wrapped one arm around her and steered Bran away from Gray-friar. "If anyone hurts you or tries to take you from me, they'd better hope God is listening. Because I won't hear their prayers for mercy."

Chapter 16

The tenement on Anchor Close loomed above McCrae, the white rags in the windows soiled from rain and smoke. The flanking tenements were so close, he could touch both sides. They banished most of the daylight, turning the close into a grave. His footsteps creaked up the wooden steps, his shadow stalking him like a monstrous imitation of Death from the devil's darkest pit.

He pushed open the door, inhaling his herbs before approaching the man in the bed. Sweat dripped down McCrae's back and face. When he removed his costume tonight, his skin would likely peel away with it. Maybe his sweat kept the plague at bay. He should scrape it into a phial and sell it with powdered unicorn horn.

"I'm McCrae."

"Jacob."

McCrae hesitated before shaking Jacob's offered hand. "Could you remove yer nightshirt so I can examine you?"

Jacob obeyed, revealing the familiar rose pattern on his skin. Every time McCrae saw it, he remembered awakening to find it on James. He blinked away scalding tears, longing for the day his memories of James no longer wounded him.

"Must you wear the mask? It haunts my nightmares."

"It keeps my nightmares away."

"Do you have any plague water? I have none left."

"Plague water won't help you." He tilted Jacob's head to check behind his ears. No buboes lurked.

"I have bathed in vinegar but it has done nothing. If I were to drink or bathe in holy water, would it cure me?"

McCrae raised Jacob's arms, checking his armpits. "The plague didn't come from God, so drinking water blessed by a pastor won't cure it."

Jacob shivered. "Did the devil send it? Is he creating Hell on Earth? Pastor Matthews says we deserve this for the immoral way we live."

"Yer not being punished, yer being infected. Could you remove yer breeches?"

"Why?"

"I need to check for buboes."

"It's improper to touch a man."

"I'm a doctor."

"Not a real one."

McCrae's jaw clenched. "The 'real' ones won't treat you."

Jacob's trembling hands unfastened his breeches and slowly pushed them down, his breathing heavy. McCrae parted the skin covering the groin and checked along it for buboes. Jacob bit his lip and whimpered, gripping his blanket.

"Am I not gentle?" McCrae checked Jacob's other side.

Jacob punched him. McCrae stumbled backwards, fell over a stool and crashed to the floor, striking his head against the hearth. Blue mist poisoned his vision.

"Shit." He pulled off his mask and held his head, groaning. Why did he accept this role?

Jacob leapt out of bed, tugging his breeches over his erection. "You had yer hands where a man has no business touching another man! It is against God!"

McCrae rose unsteadily. "That is where buboes lurk." He spat blood into the hearth.

"Because it is the cause of sin! Pastor Matthews said a touch leads to committing buggery."

McCrae laughed. "I shared a bed with my friend, James, many times when we were too drunk to find our way to separate beds. It never once led to committing buggery."

"You've lain with a man?"

"Lain *by*." He pulled his mask on.

Jacob darted to the door. "I must confess to Pastor Matthews that I allowed another man to tempt me, or the plague will kill me for my impure thoughts."

McCrae put his arm out, blocking him. Jacob crashed into it and landed on his back. "The plague does not care what lustful thoughts you harbour for men. Neither do I. But if you tell anyone, they will strangle you at the stake. Is that what you want?" Jacob shook his head. "Get back into bed or God will be the least of yer problems."

Jacob rose to his knees, praying.

McCrae covered his eyeholes with one hand. "*Sins* don't cause the plague. It's a *disease*. Next you will be telling me my lantern causes syphilis. Get back into bed."

"So you can tempt me into committing buggery?" Jacob prayed faster.

"The only instrument I wish to put in you is my lance." If Jacob was not careful, McCrae would put it through his heart, not a bubo. McCrae raised his hands. "These hands touch the dead. I'm sure you don't want them touching you." He sighed. James always seemed prepared for every situation, no matter how ridiculous. "Help me, James. What would you do?"

"Who are you talking to?"

"My guardian angel. He says you must get into bed and let me treat you or Hell will be unleashed."

McCrae grabbed Jacob under the arms and dragged him to his bed.

Jacob shrieked. "Yer face would seduce folk into acts of depravity. Pastor Matthews said a devil would seduce me to sin. You are a demon!"

"I'm *not* the bloody devil. But if you don't get into bed, you'll wish I was, because he's more merciful." McCrae wrestled Jacob into bed then handed him a phial containing cloves, rosemary, cinnamon and lemon. "Rub this on yer body. It's water from the Red Sea that has been blessed by Jesus. It will cleanse you of sin."

Jacob snatched it then pulled the blankets over himself.

McCrae left and closed the door behind him, signalling to a searcher. He laughed in disbelief, wishing he could tell James of that visit. He headed towards Pastor Matthews's house, disappointed to find no red cross on the door. No wonder his followers believed his lies. He knocked.

Pastor Matthews opened the door wearing a black cassock and a look of shock. "Begone devil! This is a pure house. There is no plague here."

"Stop. My mood won't tolerate it." McCrae lowered his hood and unbuckled his mask. "I wish to speak with you." He unstuck his hair from his forehead, wishing he could cast aside his cloak and breeches, but being naked before a pastor would not end well.

"My house and soul are clean. I will not allow you to infect them."

"Let me in or I'll tell that searcher to paint a cross on yer door. The watchman will lock you in and everyone will wonder why the purest man in Edinburgh has the plague."

Pastor Matthews glowered but stood aside. McCrae trailed him inside. The room was larger than McCrae and James's put together. Silver ornaments sat on the mantelpiece. A carpet covered the floor. McCrae's boots left imprints of kirkyard dirt, mouldy vegetables and excrement. He paced, watching more footprints stain the carpet.

"Stop lying about how the plague is spread. Yer terrifying yer followers."

"God decides who lives and who dies. He has decided these people should die because they are sinners. Prayer and holy water is the only way to cure them."

"Bairns have died. Were they punished before they're old enough to commit sins?"

"They were punished for the sins of their parents."

"Folk are not dying because they had impure thoughts about their neighbour, or because they stole bread to feed their starving family! They're dying because this filthy city is filled with rats and disease. You told them bathing was vanity and now the plague lurks in their dirt-stained wounds. The moment I step inside their homes I can smell the fetid odour of their decomposing flesh mixed with stale sweat and dried excrement."

"Dirt is God's will. It prevents the disease seeping into our bodies through our skin. If you wash away the dirt, you wash away the protection."

"Yet *you* are clean. The only thing that smells worse than yer hypocrisy is the folk you claim yer saving."

"The Romans indulged in bathing regularly. They also indulged in unholy acts at their bathhouses."

"Edinburgh's folk will not start fornicating with each other because they washed."

"People are dying because they do not follow God's word."

"They're dying because they believe *yer* lies over *my* medical training. Will you have Edinburgh die to prove God is all–powerful, all–judging? Or will you hold yer tongue and let me treat them?"

"Prayer is the only way for them to enter Heaven once this plague has taken them. Plagues are in the Bible. I suggest you stop reading your medical books and start reading the Bible. Maybe then you will cure them. Dressing as a demon from Samhain likely encourages them to sin. God is sending a message."

"So am I! If my patients die because yer telling them they're being punished, I will see you hanged at the Tolbooth for murder. See if God will show you mercy."

"I am saving their eternal souls!"

"I'm saving their *lives*. Which do you think they care for more? I'm warning you, Pastor. I will march into yer meeting-house and hang you from the cross which you preach beneath. Then I will tell yer followers I'm a messenger from God sent here to cure them. Don't make me a liar, Pastor. If I lose patients because they listened to you, I'll dump their corpses outside the meeting-house. God isn't the only one who can make grand spectacles."

"When you entered the Craft, you signed the Covenant, as all surgeons are required, yet you and James Lowther have not attended a service since you took this role. And now you stand before me, ordering me to ignore God's will."

"The pest is *not* God's will. God cannot cure them."

"If God cannot heal them, who can?"

"Me." McCrae slapped a phial of the same ingredients he had given Jacob onto the table. "Wash in this. Bless it if you must, add holy water to it, I don't care. But when you survive the plague, know that it was *not God* who saved yer life."

McCrae left, the door banging shut behind him.

A man shuffled past, flagellating himself and praying. McCrae growled and snatched the whip. He thrust a phial into the man's hands.

"I'm a messenger of God. Bathe in this to rid yerself of the plague."

McCrae spied Katrein leaving a tenement. Hamish stood outside, crouching to pat a black cat. McCrae trotted over, tossing the whip aside.

"Taming cats as well as the dead, Hamish?"

"You cannot tame a cat, Doctor Death; they possess more intelligence than all the council put together."

Katrein's raven hair hung loose around her face. She usually tied it up to prevent it annoying her when she treated people. Though half of it worked its way free after an hour. She smiled tentatively then moved towards the next tenement.

"Do I not get a kiss? Has my mask finally scared you away?" McCrae raised his hand, the mask dangling from his fingers. "Or perhaps I smell of dead folk."

"You smell of dead folk and bergamot." Hamish stood and glanced at Katrein.

The cat pounced on a piece of bread. McCrae brushed Katrein's hair behind her ear. His hand froze. Purple bruises painted her cheek. Her lip was swollen, black skin staining beneath her eye like ink had spilled onto her face.

"Kat–"

Katrein pulled away, scraping her hair down so it covered her wounds. "It was a wee accident."

"Who did this to you?"

"My patient was in pain and struck me. He meant no harm. It's part of being a nurse. And if you suggest I give it up, I will give you a matching bruise. I have no wish to be a servant girl or to work on the market or become a prostitute. And I do not wish to stay in our home all day once we are married."

"Yer a wonderful nurse. I would never ask you to quit." McCrae grabbed her hand and pulled her gently towards him, hating how she flinched. "Those are not the wounds of an accidental strike from a violent patient."

"I don't wish to speak of it."

"Hamish, do you wish to speak of it?"

"I don't want her knee in my loins."

"Kat, please." McCrae's voice broke. "I'm not leaving yer side until you tell me who hurt you." He held her arms. "Do you wish for me to frighten yer patients along with my own?"

She refused to meet his eyes. "The man I kicked in the groin dragged me into a close and tried to…rape me. I fought him off then Hamish found me. I held my candle to that scum's groin for the disgusting things he wished to do to me."

Cold seeped through McCrae's costume, freezing his veins and killing his heart. He could not breathe. His stomach clenched, nausea choking him.

"Where is he? I'll kill him!"

"He's at the bottom of Gray-friar's pit," Hamish answered. "Likely he is dead by now. If not, he'll wish he was."

"You buried him alive in a pit?"

"Aye. If I swing for it, I'll swing with pride."

"I hope his death was slow, painful and terrifying. I will make sure you don't swing."

"How? The council will have you swinging beside me."

McCrae kissed Katrein's head. "Why did you not tell me?"

"James has just died. Yer trying to rid Edinburgh of the plague and yer fighting with the council. I didn't want to add to yer troubles."

"Yer not a trouble, yer my betrothed. I wish I had got to him first. I could have infected him, given 'the plague doctor' a new meaning; become the monster folk think I am."

"Alex…he said Andrews sent him."

McCrae's eyes blazed. "I'll kill him!"

"I cannot sleep. Every time I close my eyes I see him, smell him, hear his cruel words, feel his terrifying weight on my body. He tried to touch me like no man besides you is allowed to touch me. I was scared had he succeeded, you would no longer want me for yer wife." She cried against his chest.

THE MALIGNANT DEAD

His heart ached at her pain, her nightmares, and her fear that he would reject her if that scum had stolen what no man had any right to steal.

"I love you for who you are, for how you make me feel. I don't care if I was not the first man to have lain with you, as long as I am the last. I should give him James's potion to bring him back to life so I can have the pleasure of killing him myself." He slipped a blade from his pocket and placed it in her hand. "Since the council started threatening me, I have become cautious. If any man touches you, stab him until he dies a thousand deaths. If anyone ever hurts you, he will answer to me. He will pray you kill him first."

Chapter 17

"We have a problem."

"How many times must I tell you not to come here?" Fergusson grabbed Andrews's arm and dragged him inside, shutting the door before anyone could see. He had half a mind to throttle Andrews. "What if Douglas or Kilbride had been here? Kilbride has a conscience as big as Scotland, but fortunately for us, his cowardice is bigger than England. I will not have my good name sullied by being associated with the likes of *you*."

"I checked you were alone. In my work, if yer not careful, yer dead. You weren't at the Tolbooth and it's a matter of urgency. If yer so concerned about yer 'good name' then have no dealings with me at all. *You* sought *me* out."

Fergusson sighed. "This had better be important – I was about to have my supper."

"Wallace has disappeared."

"Who?"

"The man I sent to frighten Miss Reid. I haven't seen him since."

"He probably drank himself into a stupor. Or is using the money I supplied to work his way through the brothels. You will probably find him between some whore's legs."

"I have looked in his usual places. Even the whores haven't seen him. Something has befallen him."

"I certainly shall not grieve for him. Did he do as you bid?"

"Miss Reid is not as bonny as she was two days ago." Andrews smiled. "Hopefully it will have knocked the feistiness from the bitch too."

"You said he would *frighten* her, not *hurt* her!"

"McCrae will only take heed if he fears for her safety. Don't grow a conscience now, it does not suit you."

"How badly is she hurt?"

Andrews shrugged. "She's a wee bit bruised. Wallace enjoys his work and often gets carried away." He smirked. "I would not be surprised if McCrae no longer has a virgin bride."

"You *idiot*!" Fergusson struck him on the shoulder. "If McCrae discovers who is responsible he will be after our blood!" Fergusson threw up his hands. "Why must I deal with cowards and fools?"

"If McCrae knew, I'd be cut open on his table, my insides on my outside."

"He must never learn of my involvement." Fergusson walked towards the door.

"But Wallace is missing." Andrews followed him.

"With any luck, he fell into the Nor' Loch and drowned amongst the shit and the witches. Dead men cannot tell secrets."

"What should I do if McCrae finds out we're behind the attack?"

"'*We*'? Wallace is *your* man. I merely told you to frighten her. For your sake, you had better hope McCrae does not find out. If Wallace reappears…get rid of him."

"He's my friend."

"Scum like him don't *have* 'friends'. He can hang us both. Or would you prefer to dangle at the end of a rope?" Fergusson opened the door. "Goodnight, Andrews."

"Goodnight, sir." Andrews tramped out.

Fergusson shut the door, fighting the urge to slam it. He should have hired someone more competent. Andrews was becoming arrogant. Who did he think he was? Coming to his home uninvited, where anybody could see him? Fergusson paced. If Andrews started making trouble, he could disappear too. What was one more corpse in a city full of them?

***

McCrae entered the Tolbooth and stormed up to the council office. He knocked and walked in, surprised to see Fergusson's chair empty. He removed his mask. There was no point keeping it on if Fergusson wasn't there to annoy.

"I have come for my wage."

"You cannot walk in here, demanding money, like a highwayman accosting a king's carriage," Douglas said.

"Do you see a blade in my hand, or a horse wandering yer office? I'm asking you pay me the money you promised."

"You have not cured the plague."

"If you think you can do better, you may have my herbs, my wage and you may even wear my costume." McCrae marched forwards and flung the mask onto their desk. Herbs scattered over the councillors' papers.

Kilbride jumped and pushed the mask away with his quill. "There is no need for rudeness."

"Why did you offer such a high wage? Because nobody wanted the role? Or because you hoped I'd die like Petrie? Dead men have no use for coins."

Kilbride's eyes widened, his quill slipping from his fingers. "Of course not! It is a horrible role, it deserves a high wage."

"Yet you have paid me nothing."

They exchanged glances.

"All I want is forty shillings to repay my debt to Mr Lowther and enough to buy herbs."

"Well—" Douglas began.

"Or will Fergusson forbid it?"

They shared another worried look.

"I thought the council were equally powerful. Clearly Fergusson is in charge and you two are his puppets."

"Now listen here, vagabond." Douglas stood. "First you show bad manners, now you are showing contempt. One more word and I shall have you thrown out and you will not see a penny of your wage."

"I haven't seen a penny of it anyway, so I have nothing to lose by speaking my mind. If you throw me out, I will quit. And I will tell folk what a disgusting, fear-filled, high-risk task it is for no money. I will tell them how folk they have known their entire lives will avert their eyes and step away so they do not have to touch them. How the mere sight of them will make their neighbours lock their doors. How their wives will no longer share their bed because they will come home stinking of pus and rotting flesh. How even the hangman does not cause as much fear and disgust as the plague doctor. How day after day they will put everyone they know on the death cart after watching them decay a wee bit more each day. Then I will wish you luck in finding my replacement." He snapped off a salute.

"I'm sorry McCrae, but money is in short supply," Kilbride said. "There is no trade. Once the plague is cured, trade can return then the money will be yours."

"Have you found money to pay yerselves?" McCrae laughed and shook his head at their silence. "Because sitting in a nice, safe office, discussing folks' wages and hanging the healthy is far more deserving of a wage than treating the sick. I'll return when the master is here." He snatched his mask and walked towards the door. Douglas's finance page fluttered to the floor. McCrae opened the door then looked back. "My friend is James Lowther, son of the eminent London doctor George Lowther. Should anything befall me, James will alert his father and you will feel the sword of justice on yer cowardly necks."

"Are you *threatening* us?" Douglas glared.

"Fergusson is one man. There are two of you. You don't have to dance to his tune." He imitated controlling puppets on strings. He imagined James would have laughed then slapped him across the head for his blatant contempt. His fists clenched as he fought the heat in his eyes. James may not be a ghost, but he still haunted him.

"You have no business speaking to us like that." Douglas bristled. "We have done nothing."

McCrae smiled wryly. "Exactly. Oh and tell Fergusson if he ordered Katrein's attack, I will hang him, after I have shown him how rotten he is on the inside."

***

The door banged shut. Kilbride jumped then smoothed his moustache. Horses' hooves clipped past outside the window. Market traders shouted their wares, but they lacked the passion of past traders. Some had never run a market stall before and were forced to take over after the plague visited their family.

Douglas flopped into his chair. "McCrae is becoming a problem."

"He is right. He has been the plague doctor for weeks without a penny. We would not tolerate that, yet we expect him to. He is *actually* curing people."

"We should never have offered that damn wage." Douglas rested his elbows on the desk, clasping his hands before his mouth. "It will be our ruin. We should not have listened to Fergusson."

"Maybe we *could* pay him a portion. Fines from deserters have brought in some money. Fergusson never needs to know."

"How will we pay the gravediggers? The barrowmen? If they do not get their wages, they will refuse to do their jobs. We will have bodies rotting in the street. The smell is bad enough now."

"If McCrae quits, there will be far more bodies for the barrowmen to collect, for the gravediggers to bury. Edinburgh should set an example to the rest of Scotland. Imagine the uproar if it was discovered we did not pay our plague doctor."

"What if Fergusson finds out?" Douglas arched his eyebrows.

"McCrae is right. We should be equal. We have often disagreed with him, but have said nothing."

"Do you wish to find yourself visited by Andrews's friends armed with knives and evil intentions? You have a wife to protect. I saw McCrae's betrothed yesterday, Nurse Reid. She has taken a beating. Do you wish that fate to befall Mary? Do you wish to explain to her it was your fault some ruffian attacked her? How will you look each other in the eyes?"

Kilbride sat back. "There are many vagabonds prowling Edinburgh. Just because Miss Reid fell foul of one does not mean Fergusson was responsible."

"McCrae believes he is."

"Miss Reid visits patients at night, alone, and rides with her cousin in his death cart. She is no stranger to peril."

"I find it strange that after McCrae has made demands, his betrothed is attacked. Fergusson knows dangerous people. We would be wise to keep on his good side."

"If we turn a blind eye to this, what does that say about us?"

"That we know what is good for us."

"That we are his puppets, like McCrae said."

"On your head be it should anything befall Mary."

Kilbride twisted his fingers in his lap.

Douglas scowled. "With this plague and lowlifes taking over Edinburgh, it has become a dangerous city and

I for one do not intend to end up as another name in the council's death ledger."

Chapter 18

McCrae stopped outside the school. Bairns held hands and walked in a circle.

"Ring a ring of roses, a pocket full of posies. Ashes, ashes, we all fall down." They fell to the floor.

He shivered. Bairns' singing would haunt nightmares. The plague was not only a horrible disease; it was becoming a chilling legend celebrated through song.

A lad pointed and screamed. "Doctor Death!"

"No! Wait." McCrae lowered his hood and tried unbuckling the mask.

Terrified shrieks, pointing and cries of 'Doctor Death' rang out across the playground. Bairns ran towards the school. One lad fell over. The others trampled him.

"What the devil is going on?" A teacher helped the lad up then strode towards McCrae. "You are frightening them!"

"I'm Doctor McCrae." McCrae wrestled the mask off and pushed his hair upright. "I was asked to talk to them about the plague."

"I hope you weren't planning on wearing that." He pointed to the mask.

McCrae hesitated then smiled. "Of course not."

The teacher gave him a stern look then opened the gate and led McCrae inside to the headmaster's office.

"McCrae." He offered his hand.

"Kincaid." The headmaster shook McCrae's hand. "You're younger than I expected. Have you qualified?"

"Not yet. Qualified doctors didn't want the role."

"Come this way." Kincaid led McCrae to a classroom.

A small lad saw the mask and screeched. "Doctor Death!"

"Perhaps you could leave your mask in my office," Kincaid said.

"I could explain it to them, stop them being frightened."

"To be honest, the mask frightens me. In their eyes, you are the bogeyman." He faced the class. "Doctor McCrae has kindly agreed to come and talk to you about the plague. Do not be afraid of him. He is a nice man who helps people." He smiled at McCrae. "Do you have experience with bairns?"

"I have treated them for the plague."

Kincaid frowned. "They scare easily."

"I have dissected corpses before my fellow students and eminent doctors. I think I can speak to bairns." He smiled at them and held up the mask. One lad burst into tears.

"Do you grind folks' bones and fill the beak with them?" a boy asked.

"No! It protects me from the plague. The beak holds herbs to keep the bad smells away and the eyeholes let me see. My breeches and cloak protect me from dirt. My gloves and stick let me examine folk without touching their infected skin. You may have heard that God sent the plague to punish sinners. That is a lie. God didn't send the plague. Good people get infected. The most important thing you can do to stop catching it is to keep yerselves and yer homes clean. Who can tell me what the symptoms of the plague are?"

Wide eyes stared at him. He walked to the board and picked up a piece of chalk. Bairns' names were listed on the board. Some had been crossed out.

"Why are some names crossed out?"

"The plague took them," Kincaid said.

McCrae nodded then faced the class. Empty desks sat amongst the bairns. "How do you know if someone has the plague?"

Loud ticking echoed through the room. McCrae looked around, but failed to spot the clock.

An older lad at the back raised his hand. "You die and they toss you on a cart then throw you in a pit."

"Aye, but before that happens, how do you know if you have it?"

"You're supposed to be *allaying* their fears," Kincaid whispered.

"They may have seen someone they know put on the cart. Now is not the time to pretend death does not exist. Would you rather I tell them their parents haven't died, but a unicorn has taken them away to a magical land?"

"What's the unicorn called?" a blond lad asked.

"I want to see the unicorn!"

"Can we go to the magical land?"

McCrae shook his head. "There is no unicorn. When you die, the *cart* takes you to the pit, not a unicorn." More bairns cried and asked to see the unicorn. "That song you sing. Ring a ring of roses. Having what looks like roses on yer skin is one of the signs." He wrote *rose pattern on skin* on the board. "My mask has the pocket full of posies – the herbs. These stop me breathing in the disease and it covers the worst of the smells. That is why yer parents hang herbs around yer home. Another sign is fever – shivering, feeling cold yet yer body is hot." He wrote *fever* on the board. "Coughing is another sign." He added *cough*. "Some folk have lumps behind their ears, under their arms or in their groin, wherever there are glands. Those lumps are called buboes." He scrawled *buboes – behind ears, under arms, in groin* on the board.

"My mam said you poked my uncle Fred with a stick and pus and blood burst out of him," a brown haired lad called out. "And then you burned him with a poker. She said he screamed like a baby."

The bairns' eyes widened.

"That is called lancing the buboes. It rids them of infection. The poker heals the wound."

"Does it hurt?" a lad with spectacles asked.

"Aye. But not for long. If you sit still, it does not hurt as much. Another sign is when yer fingers, toes, lips and nose turn black. It's called gangrene. Does anyone know why this happens?" The bairns' gazes didn't waver from him. "It's because yer body is dying around you. When you die, yer body rots. With the plague, it rots while yer still alive."

"Thank you for coming, Doctor McCrae," Kincaid said loudly.

"I haven't finished."

"I see no reason to terrify them further."

"I'd like to examine everyone."

"I'd have to insist that you don't wear the mask."

"It protects me from the plague."

"Look at them, Doctor McCrae."

McCrae glanced at the scared faces.

"Don't wear the mask."

"I might visit their homes. They won't be scared if they get used to it."

"Yer coming to our homes?" one lad with crooked teeth asked. "Are you going to put my mam and dad on the cart? With the dead?"

"I don't want my mam to die." A younger lad with pointy ears burst into tears.

"Don't kill my mam!"

"I don't want to be thrown into the pit!"

McCrae stared helplessly at them. He wished Katrein was here. She never made bairns cry.

"I don't kill yer parents. I *help* them. If they die, *then* I put them on the cart. My good friend Hamish drives a cart. His pony is called Bran. Hamish talks to the folk on the cart and sings them songs. Sometimes he lets them ride up front with him. Would you like to meet him?"

"He's going to put us on a cart and throw us in a pit!"

"I don't want to go on the cart," a redhead lad wailed.

"Are our parents going to die?"

"Not if I treat them. So when I come to yer home, like this—" McCrae put the mask on, "you know I'm there to heal them."

Bairns screamed and sobbed. One lad hid under his desk. Others fled to the corner of the room.

"I hoped bringing you here would stop them being scared," Kincaid said. "Instead, they will have nightmares."

"They can wake from nightmares. They cannot wake from death." McCrae removed the mask. "I'm going to examine you. You can help me spot signs of the plague, so you know what to look for."

"If we have the plague, will you lock us in to die?" an older lad asked.

"Nobody is locked in to die. They are locked in to stop the infection spreading. Who wants to be first?"

Nobody volunteered. McCrae sighed. Dealing with bairns was harder than dealing with the infected.

"Let me examine you," McCrae said to Kincaid. "That way they can see there's nothing to fear." Kincaid hesitated. "I cannot infect you!"

"I don't want to be locked in my home," Kincaid whispered. "Who will run the school?"

"Do you have any symptoms?"

"No."

"Then yer worry is unfounded."

Kincaid reluctantly sat. He unbuttoned his shirt and avoided eye contact while McCrae examined him. Some bairns crept forwards, others becoming braver until they surrounded him.

"Does he have the plague?"

"Can we see you burst a lump?"

"Will you lock him up?"

"Will his skin rot?"

"Will you put him in the pit?"

"Is it true you peck folk to death if they have the plague?"

"Mr Kincaid does not have the plague. I don't peck folk; I'm not a bird." McCrae smiled at them. "Who's next?"

The lad with pointy ears sat. "I'm Robert."

"Could you remove yer shirt, Robert?"

He obeyed. McCrae checked him and declared him healthy. Five bairns later, a seven year old lad sat.

"I'm Alasdair."

McCrae rolled up Alasdair's sleeves. Faint red roses coated his skin. McCrae glanced at Kincaid.

"He has the plague," he whispered.

Kincaid leapt up. "Sit back in your chairs."

Robert pointed to Alasdair's arms. "He has the plague!"

Screams, crashing chairs and shouts of 'he has the plague!' deafened the classroom.

"He needs to be taken home and his family examined," McCrae said.

Alasdair burst into tears. "You'll lock me up then I'll die and be put on the cart."

Kincaid moved to the board and put a cross by Alasdair's name. He wept. Kincaid led him out.

"He gave Alasdair the plague!" The lad with spectacles pointed to McCrae. "He *is* Doctor Death!"

"I cannot *give* people the plague! I'm not a nightmarish creature who prowls Edinburgh attacking and infecting folk."

"Alasdair is going to die!"

"He might not."

"Will you burn him with a poker?"

"Does the powdered unicorn horn come from the unicorn who takes us to the magical land?" the blond lad asked. "Does the unicorn cure the plague?"

"*There is no bloody unicorn!*"

"You told Mr Kincaid there was a unicorn."

He thought dealing with Pastor Matthews's parishioners was difficult. "Everyone sit at yer desk. Raise yer hands if I haven't examined you." Nobody raised their hands. "I will put crosses by all yer names and tell the damn unicorn not to come." He headed for the board.

The bairns slowly raised their hands. Those he had examined and declared clean, he lined up against one wall. He took three more lads to Kincaid's office where Alasdair sat on a chair, crying. Kincaid's shoulders slumped.

Kincaid wrote out their addresses and gave them to McCrae. "You should check the others. Soon I won't have a school left to run."

"I'm doing my best to save them."

"Soon there will be no city left for you to save."

Chapter 19

"Douglas and I have agreed we should pay McCrae a small portion of his wage," Kilbride said. "It will keep him from telling the town crier. If it became known that we treat the clengers better than the plague doctor, we would be lynched."

Fergusson arched an eyebrow. Kilbride shifted. His chair creaked. Suffocating silence coiled around his neck like a noose to choke his courage from him.

"When was this discussed? In a meeting I was not invited to attend? Did you make other decisions without me? Perhaps you decided it would be cheaper to toss the dead in the Nor' Loch instead of burying them? Or we should start giving out *cows* to treat the plague? Or hold meetings in the inn, so we seem like 'one of the people'?"

"McCrae visited us in your absence," Douglas replied.

"He knows you are fools who will bow to any urchin's demand."

"We have stood by your decision not to pay him. He has outlived our expectations. We do not wish to be known as men whose word has no meaning. People have lost faith in everything. At least let them still have faith in the council."

They were right. McCrae had outlived his uses. "We cannot afford to pay him one hundred pounds."

"He has asked for forty shillings," Kilbride said.

Fergusson leaned back in his chair. "If we give in to this demand, he will believe that we will bend to his every will if he threatens to tell the town crier."

"It is a small price to pay to save our reputations. He is convinced you know who attacked Miss Reid."

Fergusson would have to act fast. McCrae would come for him now. "That is outrageous! He will say anything to get money from us."

"We were lucky Petrie did not live long enough to demand the wage," Douglas said. "We will not be so fortunate with McCrae. We must pay him or he *will* ruin us. The other students were raised to respect the council and their masters. McCrae is a peasant from the market whose insolence results in regular beatings from his master. He has not learned the reward of keeping his mouth shut."

Fergusson studied his fellow councillors. When did the council become so weak? "Very well. On Friday he shall be paid."

Douglas and Kilbride exchanged surprised glances.

Someone knocked on the door.

Fergusson scowled. If that was McCrae, he would rip his mask from him and stab the beak through his heart.

Andrews stood in the doorway.

Fergusson wished he had something to stab through Andrews's heart too. Then all his problems would vanish. "What is it?"

"McCrae visited the school to talk to the bairns about the plague. When he examined them, he found some showing symptoms."

Kilbride uttered a prayer.

Fergusson tapped the desk. How many more lives would this damn disease take? "What of their parents? Are they infected?"

"McCrae's visiting their homes. I haven't heard of any infection."

The councillors shared worried glances.

"What should we do?" Kilbride murmured. "We have confined the infected to their homes, but these bairns are not in their homes."

"How many have the plague?" Fergusson asked Andrews.

Andrews shrugged. "Ten? And one teacher. The infected are in Kincaid's office, awaiting McCrae."

"Perhaps we can keep them there," Kilbride said. "Stop it spreading to the rest of the school."

"McCrae said you might not know you have it until it is too late. By that time you have infected your family," Douglas responded.

"We could send them to the Muir. Many have returned from there healthy. The Muir is not filthy like Edinburgh's streets. I believe McCrae is right about the plague lurking in the muck beneath our feet."

"The ludges are full. Despite our efforts, this wretched pestilence is still spreading and people are still dying," Fergusson said. "There are more people inside Gray-friar than there are outside its gates. If Edinburgh is to survive, we must make difficult decisions." He turned to Andrews. "Find out whether the bairns' parents are infected. Tell Kincaid to keep the bairns at the school. Nobody is allowed in or out."

Andrews hastened out.

"If this infection does not stop, there will be nobody to bury the last of the dead," Douglas said.

"Leith is faring no better," Kilbride said. "Most of the town now lives in the ludges. Soon, it will not be Edinburgh that is full of ghosts, it will be the whole of Scotland."

"No doubt the English will immediately claim it," Fergusson seethed. "The moment this city falls, they will take it again. I'm surprised they have not tried already. Perhaps it is fear of the plague that is keeping them out. At least we can be thankful for that. I fear you may be right, Douglas. We must pay someone to clean the streets. We will ask those from infected families. They can help save the city they are destroying."

The councillors sat in silence, too lost in their own thoughts to face hearing the others'. Once, this office was full of men's voices as they debated, decided and made the city great. Now their voices echoed in the empty chamber.

A knock at the door made them jump.

Andrews entered. "The parents aren't infected."

The councillors huddled together.

"What shall we do?" Kilbride said. "If we send the bairns home, they will infect their families."

"If we keep them at the school, they will infect the other bairns," Douglas said.

"They have been amongst the healthy ones for days," Fergusson said. "The others likely have it, but are yet to display symptoms." He turned to Andrews. "Leave us."

Andrews nodded and left.

The smell of the burning brimstone wafted over from the window. Responsibility clogged the air.

"What do you propose we do?" Douglas asked.

"Lock the school."

Douglas and Kilbride stared at him, aghast.

"No!" Kilbride exclaimed.

"We have no choice. They are *infected*!"

"They will *die*!"

"If we let them out, their parents will die too. Then their neighbours will die. There is barely a family that has not been touched by this horrible pestilence. We must do *something*!" Fergusson slapped the desk.

"Not *this*! I will have *no part* in this."

"Do you want bodies rotting in the street until the English invade and clear them away? We have maybe one hundred men left to defend the city. Why am I the only one willing to save it?"

"We will not be remembered as the saviours of Edinburgh! We will be called murderers."

"We will tell everyone this was McCrae's order. They will want someone to blame, so we shall give them him. Some people believe he is a demon spreading the plague. It is better than them losing faith in the council."

"This is a decision the whole council should discuss," Douglas said. "The bairns are Edinburgh's future."

"If we do not act swiftly, Edinburgh *has* no future," Fergusson said. "The rest of the council gave up their decision-making rights the second they passed the Flodden Wall. *We're* the ones who cared enough to stay. The decision is ours. Once this plague is over, most of the women will be young enough to have new babies – babies that are not riddled with the plague. Edinburgh can grow new life, but only if we cut the rot from it. This plague is a cancer on Scotland. The only way to cure it is to burn it out and build a new city on its ashes."

Douglas shook his head. "Bairns are not a tumour that can be killed for the country to live."

"Enough!" Fergusson stood, his chair crashing the floor. Douglas and Kilbride jumped. "This vile plague is *destroying* Edinburgh! We must do *something*, no matter how hard or distasteful it is. Do you realise how many bairns are in that school? Do you realise how many people each of them could infect?"

Douglas rubbed his face. "We will be lynched. I do not intend to dance the hangman's jig before my friends and neighbours."

Fergusson righted his chair and sat. "Then I propose a temporary measure: we confine them in the school and let McCrae treat them. If the healthy bairns have not caught the disease after three days, we shall send them home. That is what they doing on the Muir. The sick ones can remain in the school until they have recovered or died."

Douglas nodded. "I do not see a problem with that."

They looked at Kilbride. He twisted his fingers in his lap.

"We can set up the school as a treatment area," Kilbride eventually said. "Provide straw sacks for their beds. Once we explain to their families that this is to stop them from becoming infected, I am sure they will see reason."

Douglas dipped his quill into his inkpot and made a note in the council's ledger. "Future generations will read this and see everything we did to save this city." He blew on the ink. "They will think us heroes, making difficult choices for the good of Edinburgh. Maybe one day they shall erect a monument of us on the High Street, or put a plaque on the entrance to the Tolbooth."

Kilbride looked troubled. "I hope we have made the right choice."

"Their families will not die. What is wrong with that?"

"I do not wish us to be known as the men who killed Edinburgh's bairns."

Chapter 20

Fergusson weaved through Lawnmarket, holding a handkerchief of herbs to his nose and doing his best to avoid contact with the townsfolk. If what McCrae said about the symptoms not showing immediately was true, anyone could have the plague. An old woman walked past him, her wooden stick brushing his leg. He jumped back, pushing her. She cried out as she fell, the stick clattering to the ground.

The stalls on Lawnmarket offered different cloths for sale. There was an empty stall where the McCraes once sold their linen. Fergusson was tempted to buy leather and fashion himself a cloak. If it could keep that wretch McCrae safe from the plague, perhaps it was worth the embarrassment of wearing such a hideous garment. He would not wear that horrible beak though. Councillors did not prowl the streets dressed as demons from Hell's darkest imagination.

He glanced over his shoulder to check McCrae was not following him. No terrifying beak lurked amongst the market stalls. Someone bumped his shoulder. He stopped to berate the peasant who dared touch him. Scuffed, holed boots dangled before him. His gaze travelled up. Covering his mouth, he stepped back. A man hung above the steps on the side of the weigh-house, where they weighed butter and cheese. His purple face was swollen, his tongue protruding between his blue lips. It took a few moments for Fergusson to recognise him beneath his death mask – the cartwright they hanged for concealing his wife's infection. Someone must have rescued him from the pit and hung him up as a threat. Not someone. McCrae. Pastor Matthews had visited the council to report McCrae's threats about piling corpses outside the meetinghouse. Clearly the plague had caused the wretch to go insane and he was now using corpses to create street spectacles.

The man swayed, the rope creaking. Fergusson reeled backwards, fighting the vomit rising inside him.

The cartwright's eyes opened.

"Murderer."

Fergusson screamed and ran, knocking a woman into the street; stockings, butter and linen spilling from her basket. He glanced back as she cursed him. A man hanged from the stall selling cheese. The ten year old lass at the stall paid her dead father no attention as she shouted her wares. Hoarse moaning escaped the man's lips, his kicking feet stretching for the ground.

"Murderer."

Fergusson kept running. When he reached the end of Lawnmarket, he stopped at the Tolbooth, bracing his hand against the wall to catch his breath. He stared at the northern gable.

Fergusson's head adorned the spike.

"Oh God!"

He turned around, his shaking hands running through his hair.

Men and women hanged from almost every stall.

The cartwright's rope snapped. He vanished as he hit the cobbles.

Fergusson fled. He stopped outside a brothel, desperately trying to regain his equanimity. Nobody paid him any heed. Still, it did not hurt to be cautious. Reputation was the one thing he could not buy. He lifted his watch and watched the minute hand tick around. After half an hour, the door opened and Andrews emerged, tucking his shirt into his breeches and grinning, displaying his broken teeth.

Fergusson curled his lip in disgust. He followed Andrews, careful to keep on the opposite side of the street. When the meagre crowd had thinned, he darted across the market and pulled Andrews into an alley.

"Unhand me or I will gut you like a fish." Andrews pinned Fergusson to the wall, a blade pressed against his throat. Andrews smelled of cheap scotch, sweat and whores.

"I will see you hanged!"

"Sorry sir! I didn't know it was you." Andrews stepped back as Fergusson brushed himself down, glaring. "Yer lucky I didn't cut you. You cannot drag men into wynds and expect to escape unharmed. Many folk wish to kill me. I must protect myself."

"I cannot talk to you on the streets and I do not want you visiting my house." Fergusson lowered his voice. "I need you to get rid of a problem."

"What is it and when do you want it done?"

"McCrae. I need it done by Friday. When he learns we are not allowing any bairn to leave that school, he will come for us. *All* of us. You most of all. Especially if he were to discover it was *your* man who attacked Miss Reid. He is suspicious of my involvement. If he comes for me, I will be sure to tell him *you* were responsible. Without Wallace to bear the brunt of his rage, he will turn his fists to you. He is a ruffian. I am certain he is not above murder."

"He won't cause you any more trouble."

"I will pay you once it is done. And I want to see his body."

"You don't trust me?"

"I do not trust *him*. His friend, Lowther, has probably made a potion that imitates death. I want to be certain he is dead. The last thing I want is a visit from him in the middle of the night."

They shook hands and headed for the mouth of the alley.

Andrews stopped. "After you've seen his body, where do you want me to put him?"

Across the street, Fergusson saw McCrae emerge from a close. "Throw him in a pit with the rest of Edinburgh's problems."

***

Night's black cloak swept over the city. People headed indoors to avoid the cruelty that loitered in the shadows. McCrae left a house on Candlemaker Row and saw Hamish's cart head for Gray-friar. Hamish's lantern cast a fiery glow on him and his passengers. Katrein sat in the cart, a man propped up between them. Frowning, McCrae ran across the road and followed them into the kirkyard. Hamish stepped down from the cart and emptied it into the pit. Katrein helped him pull the man from the seat and he joined the others.

"You ride beside the dead?" McCrae asked. "They're infected!"

"We're not though, are we lass?" Hamish smiled.

"The plague is too scared of us," Katrein replied. "And Hamish smells so bad he even scares the rats away."

"Don't ride with the bloody dead!" McCrae exclaimed.

Hamish leaned over the pit. "Sorry ladies and gentlemen, you'll have to find yer own fun."

McCrae folded his arms, trying to look stern, which wasn't easy in the mask. "I don't want you catching the plague. Yer the only family I have. I don't even like you riding in the damn cart; I certainly don't want you treating the dead like puppets."

"We have never once tied string to them and made them dance," Katrein said. "We could have opened our own travelling Putrid Puppet Theatre, delighting and repulsing the whole of Scotland with our macabre act."

McCrae shook his head. "Sometimes I think I am the only sane person left in Edinburgh."

"Kat, have Doctor Death escort you home," Hamish said.

Katrein linked her arm through McCrae's as they left the kirkyard. He removed the mask. She ran her fingers through his hair, standing it up. "Have the council paid you?"

"I'll be paid 'once the plague is cured'."

"Do those thieves expect you to live off *scraps*? Rob the families yer helping? You should never have taken the role. Look what happened to John."

"A hundred pounds was too good to refuse."

"The way this plague is spreading, we won't be using it to buy a home, I'll be using it to bury you." She smiled. "Or I could become a rich landowner with my pick of stable boys."

"Riches cannot replace my company." He tickled her.

"Stable boys can." Katrein cackled then stole McCrae's mask and put it on, twirling around him. Her blue scarf floated behind her. "I'm the Birdman of Edinburgh! I'll sneak into bedrooms, pecking people to death and stealing their riches. People will cower in terror, locking their windows and praying they live to see dawn!"

McCrae laughed, caught her around the waist and took the mask. "You should wear one."

"It does not match my dress." She stood on her toes and stole a kiss. "Have the bairns recovered from their fright?"

"I don't know who spread those rumours that I peck the plague-riddled to death."

"Bairns imagine their own monsters."

"I'm visiting the school in the morning. If the infection hasn't spread, the healthy ones will be allowed to leave."

Scuffling teased McCrae's hearing. He turned, seeing darkened, deserted wynds and the occasional lantern glowing in the distance. A rat darted across the road. He steered Katrein away from lurking shadows.

A man stepped in front of them. McCrae pulled Katrein closer. She poked his ribs, frowning. McCrae loosened his grip.

"I need yer help," the man said.

"I'm escorting my betrothed home," McCrae replied.

"My wee lass has the pest."

"I'll come with you," Katrein said.

The man shook his head. "I only need McCrae."

"I'm a nurse."

"It's no task for a lass."

She glared. "Being a lass does not affect my ability to tend the sick."

"What's yer name?" McCrae asked.

"Joseph."

McCrae pulled his mask on, raised his hood and slipped his hands into his gloves. They followed Joseph across the street and down St Mary's Wynd. Grubby white rags danced outside windows, each one a flag of failure.

Joseph turned down a narrow passage and into a tenement. Unease crawled through McCrae. The only ones who knew his name were the ones he had visited. Most of them were not alive to share it.

A faded red cross marked the door. Limewash and burnt heather infused the air; fresh from clengers disinfecting the tenement after its occupants found a new home in Gray-friar.

"This family has already died," McCrae said.

"My lass and I were homeless," Joseph replied. "The council are banishing the homeless from Edinburgh. We had nowhere else to go. She's in here."

Katrein followed Joseph to the bedroom.

Pain blazed through McCrae's head. He stumbled, dropping his lantern. Black rain fizzed in his vision. The candle died, darkness swooping to conceal the horrors the night would expose.

A fist crashed into McCrae's face, bouncing off his mask. McCrae returned the blow, knocking the man down, his attacker's cap falling from his head.

"Andrews!" McCrae glared. "I swore the next time I saw you would be the last." He kicked Andrews in the ribs. "If you send one of yer men to attack Katrein again, you'll be thrown alive in the pit with him."

Andrews scrambled up and threw a punch. McCrae ducked then kicked him in the knee. Joseph emerged from the bedroom and grabbed McCrae, trapping his arms behind his back. McCrae flung his head backwards, breaking Joseph's nose. Joseph swore and wrenched McCrae's head back, tugging the mask up his face.

Andrews freed a blade from his pocket. "Yer mask can save you from the plague, but not from death. The council have no more use for you."

"I'm curing it!"

Katrein dashed into the room, pulling rope from her wrists.

McCrae struggled, grinding his boot down Joseph's shin then stamping on his foot. "Kat! Run!"

Andrews slit McCrae's throat. He gurgled, his legs weakening. Andrews crumpled, his blade skidding across the floor. Katrein stood over him, brandishing a heavy iron.

She threw the iron aside and snatched up the blade, pointing it at Joseph. "Leave or I'll carve you like a piece of meat."

"Kat," McCrae wheezed. His back scraped the wall as he fell, choking on his own blood. "Go!"

She smiled sadly. "When have I ever obeyed you?"

Joseph darted for Katrein. She thrust the blade up. He collapsed, blood pumping from his stomach. Katrein stared at the crimson blade, her skin paling. The blade clattered to the floor.

Katrein rushed to McCrae, tugging off her scarf and wrapping it around his throat. "Don't you dare die on me, Alex. Somebody help us!" His blood slipped through her fingers, turning the blue scarf scarlet.

McCrae coughed, blood spilling down his chin. "Nobody can...help us. They're...locked in." Nausea flooded him as he felt his life slipping away.

"When Andrews wakes I'll cut his heart from his body so he knows how this feels!" Tears streaked her face.

"You'll...hang."

"It will be worth it knowing he's rotting in the ground. I'd rather die than live with yer ghost."

Footsteps echoed outside. A figure appeared in the doorway.

"Help us! Somebody tried to murder him!"

"Why am I surrounded by fools?" The figure entered the house and kicked Andrews's side.

"Fergusson!" McCrae rasped. "Katrein, run."

Fergusson tugged Katrein up by her arm. "You are not supposed to be here. But seeing as you are, you must be dealt with too."

Katrein struggled, kicking him. "Help! Murder!"

Fergusson covered her mouth with his hand. She sank her teeth into his flesh. He tore his hand free and slapped her across the face. Her nails gouged wounds in his cheek. Fergusson struck her body. As he withdrew the blade, Katrein gasped and clutched her side. Her blood dripped onto McCrae's cloak. She dropped beside him.

"No!" McCrae struggled to his knees then fell. His world burned to ashes around him. "Katrein."

"A man who makes himself a hero, makes himself enemies." Fergusson plunged the blade into McCrae's back. "I will not be threatened by a man dressed as a bird."

Fergusson's footsteps faded. McCrae wrenched off his mask. Katrein's face blurred. He wanted her face to be the last thing he saw before Death came for him.

McCrae kissed her forehead. "Please, don't die."

He freed a phial of potion from his pocket. He poured some of the purple liquid through Katrein's parted lips then drank the rest. He kissed her lifeless lips. The liquid trickled out of her mouth and down her cheek. His touch on her arm slipped as the shadows stole him away into their lair.

Through a bloody veil, he saw Fergusson fetch the discarded paint pot on the doorstep opposite. He dipped the brush into the pot and painted a fresh cross on the open door.

Chapter 21

"Bring out yer dead!"

Since Hamish gave his bell to McCrae, his cart seemed eerily silent, as though it was a carriage of death travelling between the spirit realm and the mortal world.

A door opened on Candlemaker Row. A man carried a thirteen-year-old lad out and laid him in the cart. His quivering, rose-patterned hands adjusted the lad's coat and tucked a withering flower in his pocket. He shuffled back to his tenement and closed the door.

Hamish read the words painted on the wood. "If the Lord had mercy on yer souls, he would not take yer family." He waited, but no more doors opened. Maybe the plague was finally ending.

Or maybe there was no-one left to die.

Hamish leaned forwards and patted Bran's rump. "Last trip tonight, laddie, then we can sleep."

He flicked the reins and Bran plodded towards the kirkyard, his hooves ringing off the cobblestones. His tail flicked the flies away. Cries of 'gardyloo!' filled the night as windows opened and waste gushed onto the streets. There was no worse smell than the stench of Edinburgh when the tenth hour of the night arrived.

Hamish steered Bran into Gray-friar and stopped beside the pit. He hopped out and tipped the cart. The bodies slid into the pit.

"One day, the earth will reclaim the pit and folk will forget it was here," he told Bran. He nodded to another barrowman. "The god of death is keeping us busy."

The barrowman grunted. "There's no god here."

Hamish raised his eyebrows. "Cheerful fellow." He stroked Bran's neck. Bran snorted.

The barrowman emptied his cart.

Hamish stared in horror as a lass rolled out. "Katrein!" His blood ran as cold as the North Loch. He darted over and grabbed the barrowman's coat. "She cannot be dead! Where did you get her?"

"St Mary's Wynd." The barrowman coughed, spitting blood and pushing Hamish away. "You know her?"

"She's my cousin. She does not have the plague! She left me two hours ago. Yer mistaken. She does not belong here."

Hamish jumped into the pit, landing on the cold corpses. A guttural groan escaped the pile.

"Get out you fool, the pit's not for the living," the barrowman hissed. "You'll catch yer death and in a few days, I'll be throwing you back in. If Gregor catches you, he'll bury you in it."

"She's not dead!"

Hamish struggled to stand and scooped up Katrein. Nausea swilled in his stomach as his chest tightened. Perhaps she was merely unconscious. She was not the first person to be put in the pit alive. He touched her chest, desperate to feel her heart beat against his shaking hand.

It was still.

Grief burned his throat. "Death's not allowed to come for you, lass."

Hamish clambered out and collapsed, pulling Katrein onto his lap. He kissed her head, his tears splashing her face. The moonlight's ethereal gaze could not banish the pallor of death.

"I promised I'd look after you. I failed. Forgive me."

Hamish shook as he hugged Katrein to his chest, rocking her like he had when she was a bairn. He frowned at the wet, sticky patch on her dress then studied his crimson hand.

"This is murder!"

"There are likely many murdered folk in these pits," the other barrowman said. "Evil has a perfect place to hide with this pest."

Hamish rose and laid Katrein in his cart. He stroked her cheek then removed the rag from his face and laid it over hers. He waited for her to tear it off and accuse him of trying to kill her.

She lay as still as the dead.

Gregor marched over. "Put that body back! If you want to sell bodies to the deacon for him to cut up, you'll not take them from my pit. You think I have not noticed them going missing? Do you expect me to believe they rose from death and walked out? Go to Leith, they have plenty of corpses you can take."

"She's not a 'body'. She's my cousin and I'm burying her."

"*Katrein?*" Gregor approached the cart and lifted the rag. "I'm sorry Hamish. But the council won't allow this." He lowered the rag.

Hamish pulled coins from his pocket and slapped them into Gregor's hand. "That's my wage. Please let me bury her. I won't let her rot in a pit like bad meat thrown out from the market stalls." Gregor hesitated. "Gregor, she does not have the plague! She's been murdered. By the council, no doubt."

"You cannot make accusations like that. They'll hang you."

"Fergusson's man, Andrews, sent someone to attack her. I don't care if they hang me. As long as Fergusson and

Andrews swing beside me. Then you can sell all our corpses to the deacon. I imagine Fergusson's will fetch a shilling or two."

Gregor handed Hamish a spade. "If yer caught, don't mention me. I don't wish to join you on the executioner's stage. Someone has to bury you when they cut yer foolish body down."

"Thank you!"

Hamish led Bran towards where they buried Katrein's parents. Wiping tears from his face, he started to dig.

After an hour, he stopped to wipe sweat from his brow. Katrein stood beside the cart, her eyes wide. Bran whinnied and threw his head up. He backed towards Hamish, champing his bit.

"Ssh, laddie." Hamish patted him. "We know her." He stared at her translucent form. "I'm so sorry, Kat. Who killed you?" Her lips moved, but no sound escaped. "I'll kill him, whoever he is." She faded then reappeared. His throat burned and he rubbed his wet eyes. "Don't leave me. Yer all I have. You make my days on the cart joyful. I cannot ride that cart alone."

Katrein raised her hand, but it passed through Bran's neck. Bran whickered, his nostrils flaring. She faded again.

Hamish smiled sadly. "I knew you were too bloody stubborn to die."

***

Fergusson stared out of the carriage, fingering his scratched cheek. He had not slept, fearing he would wake to see McCrae and Miss Reid beside his bed.

Douglas and Kilbride sat opposite him, their faces grim. Kilbride clutched papers as though they contained a spell to ward off death. Fergusson studied his hand, convinced they would see the shadow of blood staining it.

The carriage stopped.

"What the devil is happening?" Kilbride leaned out the window. "Social gatherings are forbidden!"

Women crowded around the school, pleading with the men standing guard. Bairns' singing escaped the school's walls: 'Ring a Ring of Roses'. One woman smashed a window but was dragged away.

"Andrews!" Fergusson said. "What is this?"

Andrews ran over. "The mothers are threatening to knock the door down. They're begging for McCrae." He looked guiltily away.

"Let them be with their bairns."

"You said the bairns would spread the infection."

"Let them in."

Andrews returned to the men and spoke with them. They unlocked the door. The mothers pushed them aside and rushed in.

Fergusson beckoned Andrews over. "Brick up the door and board up the windows."

"Those women are healthy," Douglas said. "This is murder! We must discuss this."

"The time for discussion is over. If they wish to be with their bairns, they can die with them."

"We do not know if the infection has spread. Quarantining the bairns is a matter of necessity, but wilfully murdering mothers and bairns is not something we should be part of! This is going too far. If saving Edinburgh means sacrificing our humanity, our consciences, it is not worth it. Those women will give birth to the city's future. How can it hope to survive if we kill the very women who will bear it new life?"

"We are not doctors. We cannot tell if they are infected. I will not risk my life for some snotty-nosed bairns. It is too late for you to develop a conscience now, Douglas. The devil is already warming his fires for your soul. Andrews, brick it up."

Andrews glanced at the school.

"Now! Before I lock you in with them." Fergusson tapped the carriage's roof. The carriage jerked away. "They cannot waste their tears on the infected when the city is at risk!"

Kilbride's brow creased. "They are concerned about their bairns."

"Our priorities are saving the healthy, not troubling our consciences on those who will die within three days. Difficult decisions will not earn us friends but it will save Edinburgh."

"Not if we are damning the healthy with the sick."

"You agreed to this."

"As a temporary measure."

"It became permanent."

"Douglas is right. How will Edinburgh grow new life if the women are locked in to die? Life cannot grow from corpses."

"When the wealthy return, *they* shall give birth to the new Edinburgh."

Kilbride and Douglas shared disconcerted glances. Fergusson sighed. Why must this city be run by the feebleminded?

"A barrowman by the name of Hamish Reid saw his cousin, Katrein Reid, in a pit," Douglas said. "He's crying murder. He pulled Miss Reid from the pit to prove it. First she was attacked, now she is dead. Another barrowman claims he saw McCrae and Miss Reid heading for St Mary's Wynd with a man of ill repute last night. Nobody has seen McCrae since."

Fergusson's heart raced. "You cannot trust the words of barrowmen – they choose to ferry the dead. McCrae has probably quit as he threatened. Maybe he has been called to treat the people in the ludges."

"He is not at his lodgings, or the deacon's house. He would have quit weeks ago if he had a mind to. No other man would work that job for seven weeks without pay. He may have fallen foul of the person who attacked his betrothed."

"Why are you concerning yourself with his whereabouts? Do you have rose-patterned skin you wish him to check?"

"No!" Douglas cleared his throat. "What should we do about Reid? If he keeps shouting 'murder!', people may believe him. He is a popular fellow in the inn and Miss Reid was well-liked by her patients."

"Hang him for concealing Miss Reid's infection."

Kilbride gaped. "We should *save* the healthy. Not *hang* them. This is going too far!"

"Reid rides with the dead. He has been in the pit. He is probably infected."

"All the barrowmen ride with the dead. Do you propose we hang them all? What about the gravedigger? He spends all day with infected corpses. Shall we hang him too? And leave the corpses in their homes like gruesome mausoleums? At least then we will not have to pay the barrowmen or the gravedigger. Perhaps we should hang McCrae. He spends the most time with the diseased. Or do you suggest we burn Edinburgh to the ground and all the people with it? The infection cannot spread if everyone has died."

Uneasy silence became the fourth passenger in the carriage.

"We shall find McCrae and send him to the school," Douglas finally spoke. "Maybe he can cure them."

"McCrae knows we will pay him on Friday, so if he is yet to appear by then..." Kilbride glanced out the window. "I suppose we must find a new plague doctor."

***

Beneath the diseased bodies, something stirred.

Corpses shifted as McCrae woke from his resting place. A woman's glassy eyes stared at him, her blistered face and blackened lips close enough to kiss. A man's rotting arm embraced him. McCrae slipped his fingers beneath Katrein's scarf. The blood had dried. He touched his chest, but felt no heartbeat.

McCrae laughed. "James, you *are* a genius."

He moved the woman aside and plucked the man's arm off his chest. Pus trickled down the man's neck. McCrae sat up, spying his mask. He threw it out of the pit then pushed a body off his legs.

"Katrein!" He turned a woman over, but it wasn't her. He rolled bodies away, swearing when his fingers burst a bubo on a woman's neck. No putrid smell escaped with the pus.

Perhaps Katrein didn't die.

The moon cast a ghostly shroud over the kirkyard. McCrae removed his gloves. His hands were the colour of dead flesh. Faint roses decorated his skin. His vision blurred as blackness swooped. Earth showered him as Gregor buried the dead.

McCrae struggled out of the pit, pushing lifeless limbs aside. Soil cascaded from his cloak. Gregor prayed, brandishing his spade. McCrae snatched up his mask. It felt strange not looking through the eyeholes at the pestilent. He buckled it around his face and raised his hood before staggering towards the gate.

"I thought you were dead!" Gregor called.

"The dead have risen."

Chapter 22

McCrae stumbled along Candlemaker Row, his dead limbs struggling to remember how to move. Tallow from the candle makers no longer perfumed the air. A rat darted from an alley and stopped in front of him. It sat up, sniffing, its whiskers twitching. As McCrae passed, it bounded after him.

White rags and red crosses turned the narrow streets and wynds into a labyrinth of horrors. Everywhere McCrae looked, Death lurked. A lantern glowed like hellhounds' eyes, waiting to feast on the souls of the damned.

Another rat ran out of the shadows. McCrae removed his mask, expecting to feel the wind on his face. He felt nothing. He replaced his mask and walked on, his boots scuffing the cobblestones. He passed James's lodgings and glanced up. In the grimy window, the living dead plant hung its withered head, its leaves drooping. McCrae saluted it.

Scuttling plagued him, as though he was being stalked by a thousand demons. Black rats loitered, their eyes crimson orbs. He walked backwards and they followed. He stopped. They imitated him, some sitting on their haunches. The first rat ran up his leg and sat on his shoulder.

Voices filled the night as men returned from the inns. McCrae ducked into an alley, the rats following him.

Inexplicable fear consumed him that he was more in danger now he was dead. He waited until the men passed before emerging onto the empty street, the rats shadowing him. He glanced down every wynd, convinced he would see Andrews waiting to throw him back into the pit. He reached Hamish's tenement and knocked on the door. Weeping echoed from inside.

"Piss off!"

He knocked again.

"Get someone else to drive the bloody cart. Bran and I have seen enough death."

McCrae forced the door open and stepped over the threshold.

"Stay."

The rats vanished. The one on his shoulder ran down his body and leapt outside. He closed the door. Hamish sat by the hearth, hugging one of Katrein's dresses. His tears streaked flaming trails down his face.

"Hamish."

Hamish glanced up, his eyes swollen and red. "McCrae! I was searching for you. Where have you been?" He leapt up and pushed McCrae's shoulder. "You were supposed to walk her safely home!"

"Is she here?"

"She's *dead*!"

"No!" McCrae sank into a threadbare chair, grief ravaging his insides. "A man asked us to help his daughter. It was a trap. How did you find her?"

"I saw her roll out of the cart into the pit."

McCrae covered his mask, but no tears washed away his pain. "She was in the pit?"

"Tossed in like stale bread thrown out for the rats." Hamish collapsed into his chair. A cloud of dust escaped it. "One moment she was laughing, the next..." his voice broke, "dead. All the folk you've saved in this god-forsaken city and you could not save the lass we loved."

Grief ripped McCrae's heart into tiny pieces. Hamish was right. He had spent the past two months helping strangers, but the folk who mattered most to him were dead. Katrein's murder would haunt his conscience like a ghost wandering the ruins of a forgotten castle. Death was no longer a solace from pain. It was an eternal nightmare.

"We were attacked by Andrews and one of his men. They slit my throat. I told her to run. She would not leave me. She killed Andrews's man."

Hamish smiled sadly. "Always was stubborn."

"Fergusson came. He..." he swallowed. "Stabbed her. Then he stabbed me in the back. I gave her James's potion. So she could come back."

"She hasn't come back. Neither has Lowther. Every day I'm at that kirkyard. His bell has never tolled. The potion does not work."

"It does."

McCrae lowered his hood and removed his mask.

Hamish's eyes widened. "Witchcraft!" He leapt up and snatched a poker from beside the hearth.

"It's not witchcraft; it's science."

"What the hell are you?" Hamish backed into the hearth. "If you come any closer, I'll drive this poker through yer heart and cut off yer head." He glanced at the window. McCrae followed his gaze. Rats lined every windowsill. "The dead don't come back to life. That's against nature, against God, against *everything*."

McCrae unwound the scarf and touched the ruby necklace adorning his throat. "Andrews and Fergusson made sure I bled to death. I woke in the pit."

"If I had seen you, I would have pulled you out. Are you...dead? Are you a ghost?" Hamish jabbed McCrae's arm with the poker then backed away. "Not a ghost."

"I'm dead. But I'm alive. James achieved his dream. Maybe now he'll get his institute."

"They don't build institutes to honour necromancers. If he was alive, he'd be burned. You too."

"For curing death?"

"You haven't 'cured' death. You've trapped yer spirit in a corpse. There are legends dating back five hundred years of night-walking, plague-spreading, blood-drinking corpses. I didn't think they were real. Ghosts, aye. But not the undead. They're creatures you scare bairns with, legends only found between the pages of books; tales from the inn when the ale is flowing and the night is dark. They don't rise from a plague pit in 1645 in Edinburgh and have a conversation by the hearth. I should cut off yer head and bury you at crossroads."

"I'd rather you didn't."

"Why did Katrein not rise from death?"

"I gave her the potion too late."

"I saw her ghost. Last night. In the kirkyard as I dug her grave."

"You saw her last night? I was in the pit a *day*?"

"No wonder you have the pest."

McCrae smiled wryly. "I must be the only person in Edinburgh who got infected *after* dying. If the council knew that, likely they would have killed me long ago."

"Keep that mask on. Once someone sees you, they'll know yer not one of the living. The torture of witches will be harmless compared to what they will inflict upon you."

"I really am Doctor Death now."

Hamish lowered the poker. "I could not bury her without you. I had the wake alone. All night I cradled her as I waited for yer return."

"Where is she?"

"In her bed."

"James left me money for herbs. She shall have a coffin."

Hamish nodded. "What will you do now?"

"Avenge our murders."

***

THE MALIGNANT DEAD

Kilbride stepped out of the Tolbooth. Ponies, traps and the barrowmen's chilling calls punctuated the night. Cloaked in moonlit silver, St Giles Kirk looked less like a place of worship and more like a palace of the damned.

Kilbride walked the empty streets, smoke from his tobacco pipe teasing his nostrils. He neared Mary King's Close. White rags fluttered above him. Before they were cries for help. Now they hung like flags of surrender. A black cloak disappeared into the street.

Low groans rumbled from tenements. The city was safer with the diseased locked away. That was what he told himself when his sins kept him awake.

Footsteps stalked him. He turned. High Street was deserted. He hoped Fergusson's pet wasn't skulking in a doorway. Douglas was right – Edinburgh was a far more dangerous place when you stood on Fergusson's bad side. Kilbride pulled his collar up as though it could ward off evil as well as the cold.

Hoarse singing drifted through the silence.

"Ring a ring of roses."

Kilbride whirled around, his lantern casting disjointed monsters on the cobbles. A cloaked figure lurked near a tenement. Kilbride's chest tightened. The figure turned, St Andrew's white cross on his cloak bright in the gloom. Kilbride chuckled. Spooked by a clenger.

A cart passed, pulled by a grey pony. The driver wore a hooded cloak. And a beaked mask. The eyeholes bored into Kilbride's tainted soul.

Kilbride ran down High Street, turning left under the archway onto Carubber's Close. The night swallowed him. His heart pounded. Red crosses shamed some of the doors. He hastened down the slope, ignoring the coughs, cries and screams of his neighbours, his friends. He climbed the steps to the top floor of the tenement and shut his door behind him, his shaking hands forgetting how to work the lock. Menace prowled the streets. He placed his lantern on a table near the door.

A raspy voice whispered from the shadows: *"a pocket full of posies."*

Dread slithered through Kilbride's veins, coiling around his heart and scaring his courage away.

"Mary, is that you?" His voice quivered.

Kilbride fumbled for the lantern, knocking it to the floor. It smashed, the dark suffocating the flame.

A hooded figure with a long hooked beak guarded the hallway.

Kilbride leapt back. His pipe dropped to the floor. The figure stepped forwards, his eyes bloodshot.

"Aaaaaashes, aaaaaaashes."

The sweet aroma of herbs and bergamot oil permeated the air, cloaked with Death's scent. Kilbride groped for the door, inching it open. It banged shut. The figure wrapped his cloak around him, his festering skin pressing into Kilbride's face.

"We all fall down."

Kilbride clawed his throat as it closed, choking him. He coughed, blood spattering the floor as his oesophagus shredded. Fear eroded his senses, the stench of his rotting skin making him vomit violently as he became interred in his living tomb.

Chapter 23

Fergusson's footsteps reverberated through the corridor as though his wraith stalked him. His fingers brushed the peeling walls, guiding him through the gloom. Unease stalked him; the unsettling feeling of being alone in a building that was usually full of life. Piercing scratching tormented him. He peered into the classroom. Bloodied words appeared on the board beside the bairns' crossed out names:

MURDERER

A ruby bead snaked down the board and dripped onto the floor. Drip. Drip. Drip. Groaning haunted his ears. Fergusson stopped, loath to face the fiend creeping through his nightmares. Chastising his foolishness, he turned. A blue flame weaved towards him. The dead shuffled after it. Pus seeped down their rose-patterned skin, their blackened fingers reaching for him.

"Murderer."

Fergusson ran, his heart beating to every stride. A shadow flitted past a door, its hooked beak silhouetted. He pressed himself against a wall, his chest constricting. Maybe the superstitious were right.

Maybe the dead walked this earth.

He risked a glance. The shadow vanished. He scuttled down another corridor. Bairns blocked it, tears staining their decaying faces.

"Murderer." They pointed, moving towards him.

The school was no longer a place where lads learned.

It was a prison where they died.

Terror tightened its fingers around Fergusson's throat, trying to silence him. The bairns circled him, joining hands and skipping around.

"Ring a ring of roses, a pocket full of posies. Ashes, ashes, we all fall down."

Their rotting bodies crumpled to the floor.

Fergusson twisted on his heels and ran, leaping over two fallen lads. Dragging feet, agonised coughs and abject weeping echoed through the corridors as though a mournful spirit was doomed to wander the school for eternity. The blue flame hovered by the main door, beckoning as it danced to Death's drums.

He wrenched open the door.

Fergusson bolted upright in bed, his scream dying on his lips. Sweat shrouded him, his nightshirt sticking to his body. He breathed hard, his heart racing, as though his spirit was still being hunted in the nightly realm.

"It was a dream. Dreams are not real."

Wiping his face, he opened the flint box, hating how his hands trembled. It took several attempts to light the flint then ignite the candle.

Miss Reid stood at the foot of his bed.

"Murderer."

Blood spilled down her dress, flowing onto his blankets. He tucked his legs up as the blood seeped closer, staining his blankets with his dark secret.

Fergusson scrambled out of bed, tripping in his haste. Miss Reid vanished. He raised the lantern, dreading seeing that damn beak. The flame writhed to the bairns' chilling song. He whirled around, shadows swirling around him.

Galloping hooves and a horse's indignant whinny haunted the street.

"Bring out yer dead!"

THE MALIGNANT DEAD

A bell rung furiously as though announcing the end of time.

Fergusson rushed to his window, opened the shutters and looked down on the deserted Covenant Close. A black figure slipped into the shadows.

Blood thundered in his ears, as though Death's footsteps marched towards him. He leaned against the wall, summoning the courage to look again.

Nothing moved.

He turned away.

Miss Reid stood before him.

"I will not be terrified in my home!"

He pushed her, but his hands passed through her. She disappeared.

He strode back to bed and climbed in. He closed his eyes.

Tick. Tick. Tick.

His eyes flew open. The ticking stopped. He listened, his fists clenched. The darkness whispered secrets he was not permitted to hear. He closed his eyes.

Tick. Tick. Tick.

He opened his drawer and dropped his watch into it. He shut the drawer then waited. Satisfied, he rolled over.

Tick. Tick. Tick.

***

Fergusson and Douglas walked away from the Tolbooth. Fergusson rubbed his bloodshot eyes. Sleep was no longer an escape from the horrors of the day. Darkness brought its own terrors. Although Reid had stopped crying murder and McCrae was buried in the pit, he still expected to see him at his bedside, his hideous mask leering at him in the gloom. Every time he closed his eyes, he heard that damn rhyme sung outside his window.

"What shall we do about a new plague doctor?" Douglas asked. "People are demanding to see McCrae. Soon the sick will be banging on the Tolbooth's door."

"We shall offer the wage to anyone."

"We cannot have a flescher treating the sick!"

"Most of the medical students have left. McCrae and the Lowther lad were two of the few who stayed."

"What about Lowther?" Douglas suggested. "People respect him because of his father. He comes from a family of doctors, not linen sellers. They will not fear him like they feared McCrae."

"I have spoken with the deacon. Lowther has not been seen for some time. He likely paid the guards to look the other way while he escaped to London, sneaking McCrae out with him. The deacon said they were inseparable. We will offer the wage to anyone who will take the role. I will not allow Edinburgh to be laughed at because we cannot find someone to treat the infected."

Douglas sighed. "We should have paid McCrae. Maybe we would still have a city to save."

"It is too late for regrets."

Andrews ran over. "Kilbride's dead!"

"*What?*" Douglas demanded.

"His wife's screams woke the street. They're collecting him now."

Exchanging perplexed glances, they followed Andrews to Kilbride's tenement. Dread strangled Fergusson's heart. If this was murder, he would see Reid hanged. They stood higher up Carubber's Close as two barrowmen heaved Kilbride's plague-riddled body onto the cart. A red cross on his forehead trickled blood into his eyes.

"Why did he not say he was infected?" Fergusson seethed. "He has put us at risk!"

"Sometimes you do not know until it is too late," Douglas murmured.

"*This* is why we hang those who conceal their relative's infection. I knew I should not trust him."

"He was our friend. Show some respect."

A searcher hung a white flag from the window then slathered red paint over the door.

"I'm clean!" Mary shrieked from inside.

"Yer husband died of the plague. You must be quarantined," a watchman answered.

Mary edged past the watchman. "No, please. He wasn't sick!"

The watchman pushed Mary inside and locked the door. Mary pounded on it, begging for mercy, but with the dead outnumbering the living, the city could no longer afford mercy.

Fergusson and Douglas stepped back as the cart rolled past, the grey pony flicking its tail. The barrowman watched them over the black rag covering his face. Their lanterns cast cruel shadows on to the cart, turning their friend into a monster. Kilbride's blotchy, blistered face stared at them from the pile. Large seeping buboes blighted his neck. His terrified eyes had seen beyond death's veil.

Fergusson shuddered. "We must replace him."

"There are barely enough healthy men for military duty, let alone council duty," Douglas replied.

"Then we shall leave Edinburgh and return once the infection dies. We shall build a new city from its ashes."

"People will tear us limb from limb!"

"They are locked in their homes. Those who are not can be dealt with. We were foolish to stay. I thought we could save Edinburgh, but I see now it is damned. Gather your belongings, unless you wish to die amongst the diseased. Soon, we shall be rid of this city and its cursed dead."

***

Darkness cloaked the city, providing a dungeon where demons could play without witnesses. Hamish lurked in the shadows, his rag concealing his face. Bran's ears twitched. He raised his head and snorted, his breath spiralling into the air like the smoke created when a witch was burned for her sins.

Hamish shifted, the cart seat creaking as he watched the inn across the road. Footsteps scuffed towards him.

"Yer enough to scare the devil away, birdman."

"Good."

"Douglas and Fergusson are leaving Edinburgh. Kilbride's death has shaken them. Guess they don't want to ride on my cart. I don't know why; I'm charming company and I'd let them ride up front with me. That's not an offer I grant everyone."

"You'd make a good spy."

Rats scuttled over McCrae's feet, up his legs and around Hamish's cart. They investigated the bodies awaiting burial, their sharp claws piercing the flesh, their noses twitching at the enticing smell of dead meat. Bran flung his head up, backing away.

"They don't pay enough attention to barrowmen to tell us apart. All they see is a man with a rag over his face sitting above the dead. They only knew my name after I cried 'murder'. They would not know Bran if he trod on their feet." Bran stamped his hoof and shook his head.

"If they're leaving, we don't have long." McCrae patted Bran, who dodged away. "You've played yer part. Thank you."

"Yer not finishing this alone. Katrein was the only person who loved me. And they took her from me. They'll suffer for that."

"I don't want you risking yer life. They cannot kill me twice. They didn't foresee me having a friend whose sole ambition was to become famous for cheating death. And raising the plague doctor from his grave."

A prostitute left the inn. She hitched her skirts over the filth, laughing as she fell against a wall.

"How do you know Andrews will be there?"

"While he was following me, James was following him. Andrews spends his blood money on ale and whores."

"Andrews didn't spot James in his fine clothes?"

McCrae smiled. "He borrowed my clothes."

Hamish laughed. "I cannot imagine that."

"He loved it. Pretended he was a spy." McCrae's eyes burned as the memory turned to ash.

Andrews skulked out of the inn grabbed the prostitute from behind and carried her down the alley. She shrieked then giggled. Seconds later, drunken grunts and moans replaced the laughter.

Hamish leaned forwards and patted Bran's rump. "The council can threaten me with the noose for all I care. I'd risk my life to avenge Katrein's murder. I have nothing left to lose."

Chapter 29

Decomposing bairns circled Douglas in the schoolyard, holding hands, skipping and singing that haunting rhyme about the plague. Their bodies slowly turned to ash.

"We all fall down."

They crumbled into piles of ashes. A breeze scattered them, swirling them like phantoms. Douglas raised his arm to shield his face, coughing as the ashes slipped between his lips and invaded his lungs. Roses blossomed on his hands. He touched his neck. Buboes erupted behind his ears. Warm pus trickled down his neck, the stench assaulting his nostrils. He coughed. Blood splattered his feet and the ground. His fingers blackened as his body rotted around him.

Whispering voices punctured Douglas's nightmares. Tapping on the window disturbed him, like the devil had come a-knocking to claim his soul. He sat up and looked to the window. Nothing but hissing blackness. He frantically touched behind his ears. No buboes. He raised his hands but the dark concealed any infection that may lurk. Something scuttled across the wooden floor. He tensed, his ears straining. The silence was too still. His heart drummed as though announcing an execution.

"It was a dream."

Douglas closed his eyes, feeling unseen eyes upon him.

Scrabbling. Clicking. Scratching.

"Ring a ring of roses," a rough voice sang.

The darkness pulsed with malevolence, as though possessed. Douglas lit his lantern.

Black rats scampered over the floor, his furniture. His bed. Their whiskers twitched as they crawled over his blankets, their long, thick tails snaking behind them. Douglas scrambled backwards, his back hitting a damp patch. He turned, his lantern spilling light onto a bloody cross on the wall. *May the Lord have mercy on your soul* was scrawled above it.

His lantern died.

"A pocket full of posies."

Douglas's breath was entombed in his throat. Something brushed his arm and he yelped. His blankets moved as the rats edged closer.

At the foot of his bed, a lantern ignited. Silhouetted in the glow, was a hooded, beaked figure. The flame danced in the mask's glass eyes, turning them into windows to Hell.

Douglas's voice shook. "*McCrae*? But you are—"

"Dead."

Douglas shook. Whiskers tickled his ankle, claws prickling his skin. Icy sweat bathed his body as a rat explored his foot. "You cannot be dead. We would have been informed."

"By who? Fergusson and Andrews killed Katrein and I. Anyone who bore witness to his heinous act will either be counting their coins or lying in the pit. Dead men tell no tales."

"Fergusson may seem harsh in his decisions but he is not a murderer."

"My stab wound says otherwise. One hundred pounds. Is that all my life was worth?"

"Kilbride and I wanted to pay you. Fergusson forbade it. Have mercy." The cold blood from the cross seeped through his nightshirt.

"Where was yer mercy when you bricked those bairns in to die?"

"They were infected! If we do not stop the plague, the entire *city* will die."

"You don't care about Edinburgh – yer leaving it."

The rats slunk closer. Douglas curled up, tugging his nightshirt over his legs.

"No!" He pushed the rats away, screeching when one sank its teeth into his hand. "We *begged* him not to lock the school but he would not take heed. What else could we do?"

"Throw him in the Tolbooth for murder. No man is too rich to die."

McCrae's boots clumped across the floor, his lantern swinging. *"Ashes, ashes."* The rats swarmed around McCrae. One perched on his shoulder, poised to jump.

"Fergusson killed you! I had no part in it."

"You stood by and let it happen. You watched while they bricked up the school. You could have stopped him. Instead you let them die. I won't kill you."

"Oh. Thank you."

"I will watch."

"No! Please!"

"We all. Fall."

The lantern died, plunging the room into darkness.

"Down."

The rats pounced. One landed on Douglas's face.

Douglas screamed.

***

McCrae sat in Hamish's cart, his elbows on his knees.

The brothel door opened and Andrews stepped into the night, whistling. McCrae's jaw clenched. He patted

THE MALIGNANT DEAD

Hamish's knee then jumped into the back of the cart and lay amongst the corpses. The rats abandoned the cart for the shadows like a surging black sea. Bran whinnied and stamped his hoof. Andrews glanced up.

Hamish flicked Bran's reins. "Bring out yer dead!"

Bran pulled the cart out onto the street. Two rats bounded after Andrews and darted in front of him. He cursed, aiming a kick at one of them. It scuttled away, unharmed.

"Stinking, filthy city," he spat.

Four rats ran on ahead into an alley. As Andrews neared it, something smashed on the ground. He jumped and peered into the alley.

McCrae's arm hung out of the back of the cart. Hamish clicked his tongue and Bran trotted on.

"Bring out yer dead!"

Andrews leapt back against the wall, clutching his chest, his legs buckling. Hamish stopped around the corner and McCrae climbed out. He crept into the shadows and waited. Andrews walked past, glancing over his shoulder. McCrae threw a sack over Andrews's head, muffling his cries for help beneath his glove.

"Ssssh," McCrae whispered. "You'll wake the dead."

Andrews kicked, trying to wriggle free, but McCrae dragged him deeper into Edinburgh's streets until they emerged at the Tolbooth.

"All clear," Hamish announced, opening the door.

They carried Andrews inside and up to the second storey roof, where the empty gallows waited. Andrews struggled, his suppressed cries becoming desperate. He grabbed the doorframe. McCrae hit his hand off and marched him to the gallows, tying his hands behind his back. He slipped the noose around Andrews's neck and tightened it.

"No, please, don't do this."

McCrae wrenched the sack off.

Andrews gasped. "*You*! But yer...dead." He stepped back, nearly falling off the stool. He choked and quickly regained his footing.

"Rumours of my death have been somewhat...overstated."

"I killed you!"

"Sometimes the dead don't stay dead." McCrae smiled. "Unfortunately you will. You cannot escape Hell."

"I was following Fergusson's orders! If I disobeyed him, he would've hanged me."

"You didn't obey him out of *fear* – you enjoyed his money. Whores aren't cheap and no respectable woman would touch you. You sent yer man to hurt Katrein. You knew what he would do to her. No lass deserves that."

Katrein's memory scorched a wound on his heart. She died because of him. That guilt would torment him long after his body rotted into the ground.

"Yer man spent his last few moments trying to escape the pit." Hamish smiled coldly. "You'll wish yer death came so easily."

"Wallace was only meant to frighten her to stop you demanding the money. You were supposed to catch the pest and die."

McCrae tied rope to each end of the gallows then untied Andrews's wrists. He pulled Andrews's arms out to the side and retied them.

Andrews struggled. "You cannot do this. They'll hang you!"

"You cannot kill what is already dead. And when I am finished, there will nobody left on the council to order my hanging."

McCrae removed a phial from his pocket and pulled the cork out. Vapour escaped, crawling around his hand like smoke from an angry dragon. Andrews backed away, his foot slipping off the stool. He gagged as the noose strangled him. He fought to step back onto the stool, his outstretched arms unbalancing him.

"My friend James was fond of making potions. It was his potions that raised me from my death. It's only fair they send you to yers. I found this one with a warning label: 'Poisonous. Do not drink'."

"Please, have mercy!"

"Where was yer mercy when you sent yer lowlife friend to rape Katrein? Where was yer mercy when you slit my throat and left me to die? I will not show you mercy; I have none left to give." He turned to Hamish. "You don't have to help."

"I held Katrein all night after Wallace tried to rape her. I dried her tears, calmed her shakes and sang away her screams. And I held her all night after she died. So I will hold this scum while you send him to his death."

McCrae pinched Andrews's nose shut and forced his mouth open. Hamish held him steady. Andrews choked as McCrae poured the liquid down his throat. McCrae and Hamish stepped back.

Andrews spat, gasping. "I'll see you in Hell."

McCrae patted his face. "Tell the devil Alex McCrae sent you."

Andrews jerked and gasped, his eyes widening as the potion burned his insides, his skin bubbling. Andrews slipped off the stool, the noose constricting. The stool clattered to the floor, rolling away. Andrews danced on the end of the noose as the poison ate him from the inside out. Screams were torn from his throat as his skin melted from his body, exposing his gruesome insides. Finally his body hung still, the gallows creaking as it claimed another life in the city of the dead.

Chapter 25

Tick. Tick. Tick.

Fergusson opened his eyes, expecting to see Miss Reid at the foot of his bed. She had been there every night since Kilbride's death, trying to inflict guilt upon his conscience. Everything he had done, he did for Edinburgh. The city would have fallen weeks ago had a weaker man been in charge.

Fergusson's room lay empty. He released his breath, silver vapour vanishing into the darkness. He swung his legs out of bed. Miss Reid lay on the floor, blood seeping from her side. Her lifeless eyes stared accusingly at him.

Fergusson wrenched his legs up. An icy chill seeped into his body. He wrapped his blankets around him, but they could not banish the coldness from his soul. Closing his eyes, he uttered a quick prayer and forced himself to open his eyes.

She had gone.

He leapt up and called for his servant to dress him.

"Pack my belongings and have a carriage ready to leave in one hour. The rest of the council have summoned me to Stirling."

The servant nodded and left to fetch his trunks.

Tick. Tick. Tick.

Someone knocked the door. Fergusson jumped then admonished himself for his foolishness.

"What is it?"

"A letter was pushed through the door, sir."

"Give it to me."

The servant entered and handed Fergusson the letter.

I have urgent business to discuss. Come to my home immediately. Douglas.

Fergusson shook his head. A matter of urgency to Douglas was probably a misplaced pipe. "Can it not wait until we are free of this damn city?"

He rushed downstairs and had the servant bring his coat. He closed the door behind him. No ghosts waited on the corner. It was unsettlingly quiet. Those damned crosses burdened most of the tenements. They seemed less like a plea for mercy from God and more like a frightening warning to the living: death is everywhere.

Fergusson ducked into a doorway whenever he heard one of those wretched carts. Any of them could be driven by that Reid fellow. Despite the reward he had offered, not one barrowman had brought Reid to the Tolbooth.

Fergusson surveyed the narrow, steep Advocate's Close. Nothing stirred; not the living and certainly not the dead.

He knocked on Douglas's door.

"You said you had urgent business." He stepped back and glanced up at Douglas's bedroom window. The shutters were closed.

Fergusson knocked again then checked his watch. He wanted to leave without that wretched scoundrel Andrews noticing. He would not allow his dirty secrets to follow him out of Edinburgh. He peered through a window, spying Douglas's trunks in the corner of the room.

"Douglas?" Fergusson pushed the door open and edged inside. Sinister silence filled the house. "The carriage will be at my tenement soon." Fergusson crept from room to room. "If you are not ready, I shall leave you behind." He entered Douglas's bedroom and opened the shutters. "Get up." He turned around.

A bloody cross mocked him from the wall above Douglas's bed, which was awash with blood and the plague-festering body of what used to be Douglas. Rats feasted on the flesh, blood droplets clinging to their whiskers. Douglas's mouth was fixed in a silent scream, his blankets hooked in his death grip.

"Dear God!"

A rat scuttled across the floor, Douglas's eyeball dangling from its mouth. It stopped and sat up, staring at Fergusson before vanishing under the bed with its feast.

Fergusson gagged then fled, flinging open the door and bolting into the close. He leaned over, coughing and gasping.

A black cloak flapped up ahead. He sheltered beside a wall. His chest tightened, his hands becoming slick. The plague had not killed his fellow councillors; it was the plague doctor. Maybe McCrae did not die. Maybe he had been hiding, waiting to seek revenge. He had the perfect cover – they could not hang a dead man.

Fergusson risked a glance. The doctor wore a brimmed hat, not McCrae's favoured hood, which made him resemble an outlaw. Fergusson ran across High Street, narrowly avoiding a grey pony pulling a cart. A black clad figure lay on the bodies. Fergusson gasped before realising it was the blacksmith.

"Get a hold of yourself!"

He forced himself to walk. It would not do for people to see him fleeing like a criminal after one of his councillors had been murdered. Once the finger of blame had been pointed, it would be difficult to remove that stain from his reputation. He would leave Douglas for someone else to find once he had escaped this decaying city.

He reached his tenement. A bloodied cross marked his door. *May the Lord have mercy on your soul.*

Fergusson's heart thundered against his ribs. His hands shook as fear charged through his body.

He marched inside. "Where is my carriage?"

THE MALIGNANT DEAD

Fergusson clenched his fists, taking deep breaths to calm the storm brewing in his mind. He would not die like Kilbride and Douglas.

"Your carriage is ready, sir," the servant said. "When should we expect you back?"

"When I am ready to return."

The servant threw his trunks onto the carriage roof while Fergusson jumped in, concealing his face from witnesses.

"Where to, Councillor?" the driver asked.

"Glasgow."

"Are you sure?"

"Is it infected?"

"No, but it's...Glasgow. That's where we banish our lowlifes to."

"Just drive!"

The driver flicked the reins and the horses trotted away. Fergusson watched the buildings pass. Would he ever see Edinburgh again? When he returned, would he be able to rebuild it? Or would it be a city of ghosts?

He had never imagined leaving Edinburgh. But he never imagined Edinburgh would fall foul to such a horrific disease.

The carriage stopped. Fergusson stuck his head out the window to berate the driver and saw the locked gate of the Flodden Wall. What example was he setting the people of Edinburgh, if even he was fleeing it?

The door opened.

Frowning, Fergusson stepped out. The driver's seat was empty. The street was deserted. Nobody guarded the gate.

"Driver? I do not have time for this! We must leave!"

The grey pony bared its teeth and stamped its hoof. Fergusson stepped back.

The houses were sealed. White rags hung still.

"Ring a ring of roses."

"Who's there?"

The horses shifted.

"A pocket full of posies."

Fergusson edged to the next street. Almost every window displayed a white rag, almost every door a red cross.

An inn sign creaked, burdened by the weight of Andrews's hanging body. Most of his skin had melted away. He was unrecognisable, except for his cap.

"Oh God, no!"

Fergusson stumbled backwards, covering his mouth. He turned around. The Flodden gate swung open, creaking.

"Ashes, ashes. We all fall down."

Fergusson fled towards the gate. It swung shut. Miss Reid stood on the other side, gripping the bars.

Something struck his head. He landed on his back, staring at a beak and glass eyes.

***

Fergusson sat up, gasping. He inhaled to calm his galloping heart. Sunlight seeped into the room through a small window.

A dusty blackboard listed plague symptoms and names. Some were crossed out, others had crosses beside them. A cane hung on the end of the board.

Dead bairns slumped over their desks, some still upright in their chairs.

"No!"

Fergusson smashed the small window with a chair, spying a board on the ground and a barrowman. "Help! I am locked in!"

The barrowman led his grey pony over.

"Were you driving my carriage?"

"The only carriage I drive belongs to Death."

"I am Councillor Fergusson. You must help me! I shall reward you handsomely."

THE MALIGNANT DEAD

"I'm Hamish Reid." He smiled. "You killed my cousin, Katrein, and McCrae. I'd rather hang you than help you."

Fergusson swallowed the nausea threatening to overwhelm him. "Where is your proof?"

"Where there's dead, there's ghosts."

"For the love of God, help me!"

"For the love of Katrein, I won't." Hamish covered the window with the fallen board. "There's no god here."

"You will hang for this!"

"Aye, maybe. But you will not be alive to witness it."

Reid nailed the board to the window frame, killing the weak sunlight.

Fergusson dashed into the corridor. Bairns and women lay sprawled along the floor. He crept past, a foolish notion in his head they may rise if disturbed.

His heart thudding in time with his footsteps, he sprinted to the front door. He tugged and kicked it. Sweat coated under his arms. His hands slipped off the handle.

Dread poisoned his heart. His footsteps echoed through the school.

"Ring a ring of roses."

He yelled as he trod on a woman's outstretched hand, her other arm cradling her son.

Fergusson ducked into a classroom and searched the desk for the keys. Bodies huddled in the corner. He abandoned his search and entered the headmaster's office. Kincaid sat in his chair, his head slumped over the back of it. His wide eyes stared at the ceiling, a quill gripped in his fingers. Dust shrouded the unfinished letter, the spilled ink from the fallen pot long dried. Fergusson ransacked the room, but failed to find the keys. He paused at the door. The door glass opposite reflected a beaked mask. Fergusson retreated into the office, breathing hard.

He peered out. The figure had gone. He crept down the corridor then held his handkerchief over his mouth and nose as he rummaged through the dead.

Heavy boots strode towards him. Fergusson's head whipped up. Muddy footprints stained the floor.

"A pocket full of posies."

Fergusson ran. The cloaked, beaked figure from his nightmares blocked his path.

Fergusson skidded to a stop. "No! You're dead!" Groaning tormented him. Scuffing feet slunk towards him. "I shall wake from this nightmare and find myself in my bed."

"Yer bed awaits you in Gray-friar."

The corpses in the corridors lurched towards him. Classroom doors opened and bairns filed out. Their decaying flesh wept pus, leaving trails on their skin. Their bloodshot eyes stared through him. Their rotting fingers reached for him.

"Murderer."

He turned. McCrae stood behind him. Black rats blocked the way. "I was trying to save Edinburgh!"

Fergusson pushed through the corpses and fled. More bodies lay where they had fallen. One woman gripped a set of keys. Fergusson darted over and snatched them, ripping off her shrivelled fingers. Gagging, Fergusson wrenched them free and flung them onto her.

"Ashes, ashes."

Fergusson tiptoed down the corridor, careful not to the wake the dead. He reached the back door and inserted a key into the lock.

A skirt rustled. He glanced over his shoulder. The dead were still. His heart hammering, he tried another key.

"Please," he whispered.

The lock would not open.

Someone groaned. He closed his eyes, muttering a prayer as he turned. He opened his eyes.

The dead were rising.

His shaking hands forced key after key into the lock. Feet shuffled towards him, accompanied by the unearthly moans of the dead.

The lock turned.

"Thank you Lord!" He wrenched the door open.

A wall of bricks stood before him.

"Oh God!"

Fergusson whirled around. The glass eyes of McCrae's hideous mask reflected Fergusson's terror. The walking dead flanked him.

McCrae tore off his mask, his blackened, blistered face greeting Fergusson, his decaying skin peeling off his bones. His dead eyes were bloodshot.

Fergusson sank to the floor, trembling. "May the Lord have mercy on my soul!"

McCrae's gloved hand reached for him.

"We all. Fall. Down."

Epilogue

Rain streaked the wooden cross marking Katrein's grave. It sank into the soil, as though the earth feasted on the world's misery and drank its tears.

The kirkyard was empty. Gregor was digging a new pit in St Giles's churchyard. Gray-friar had seen too much death.

"The council are dead. Andrews is dead. I have no purpose." McCrae stared at the grave, Katrein's blue scarf flapping around his neck. "I'm trapped in this rotting body because there's no cure for death. I have drunk every one of James's poisons, yet here I am. I asked Hamish to cut off my head. But he believes I would survive and does not wish to converse with my decapitated head." His gaze roamed the desolate kirkyard. "This time next year, we would've been married. Instead, the only flowers you'll be holding will be the ones I lay on yer grave." Every word tore his soul. Every day without Katrein hurt as much as the last. "I want to leave Edinburgh. I cannot live in a city of ghosts. Yet there are folk still suffering from the plague. They don't know I'm no longer one of the living. I vowed to remain the plague doctor until I cured it. It cannot kill me now."

McCrae crossed the darkened kirkyard to the furthest corner, where James's grave sheltered under a tree. "I hope wherever you are, yer making life difficult for someone."

McCrae pulled his hood up over his mask and trudged away from the grave. Hamish and Bran waited by the gate. Katrein appeared before McCrae. He stopped. A smile crept across his face.

"Hamish said you were too bloody stubborn to die."

Behind him, James's bell began to ring.

About the Author

C L Raven are identical twins from Cardiff who love all things horror. They spend their time looking after their animal army and drinking more Red Bull than the recommended government guidelines. Along with their friend, Neen, they prowl the country hunting for ghosts for their YouTube show, Calamityville Horror.

Their work has featured in 8 Hours Anthology, published by Legend Press; August 2010 issue of Writing Magazine (winning ghost story); The Pages Anthologies; issues 50 and 52 of Dark Fire Fiction, issues 6 & 17 of Dark Moon Digest and issue 13 of Siren's Call. They also contribute articles to Haunted Digital Magazine and Oapschat website. They have self-published six short story collections and one novel, which was shortlisted in the National Self-Publishing Awards. They have been longlisted twice for the Exeter Novel Prize with Bleeding Empire and Silent Dawn. Their short story, *Autumn of Terror* will be published in *The Mammoth Book of Jack the Ripper* by Little, Brown in Autumn 2015.

Connect with us online:
Blog - www.clraven.wordpress.com

Twitter - @clraven
@CalamityHorror

Facebook - C.L.Raven-Fanclub
Calamityville Horror fan page -
www.facebook.com/CatsTalesOfTerror

Instagram - clraven666
CalamityvilleHorror666

Acknowledgements

Many thanks to our beta readers: our mum, Lynette and Lesley for your great advice. And especially Anya, who has championed this book from its beginning as a 7000 word story (published in Dark Moon Digest Issue 17) until its creation into novella form. You all make us better writers.

Special thanks to Jo Harrington for helping us with the research of the plague and Scottish history. You helped bring the story to life. Any mistakes are entirely our own.

We'd like to say a big thank you to Ex Libris, our fellow co-conspirator and evil plotting genius. If it wasn't for your elixir idea, James Lowther wouldn't exist.

Also thanks to our editor Emma for spotting the minor errors and for working so quickly.

We'd also like to thank etymonline.com, an online etymology dictionary, which not only lists words' original meanings but also the dates when they were first used. It has been an invaluable tool in making sure the words in our book are historically accurate.

To Rhiwbina Library, thank you for sourcing the books from Scotland and buying in one of the books especially for us.

Thanks to Hayley for designing our leaflets and Wil, Laura, Mykal, Janette, Peter and Cinta for your continued support and for refusing to let us quit.

Massive thanks to River Rose for creating yet another stunning cover. You force us to make our books perfect just so they don't let the cover down. You turn our books into works of art.

Note from the authors

The Ring a Ring of Roses rhyme used in the book is a combination of the British and American versions. In the British version, it's 'atishoo, atishoo, we all fall down' but we used the American 'ashes' because it's creepier.

The idea of putting a bell above someone's grave in case they were accidentally buried alive first came into use in 1829 when so-called 'safety coffins' were popular. They were designed by Dr Johann Gottfried Taberger. We used artistic licence to fit with the story. So although they weren't in existence, Katrein could have thought of using a bell, just not patented it. How would you explain 'zombie' to the patenting office?

As research, we read two books by Helen Dingwall: *A Famous and Flourishing Society: The History of the Royal College of Surgeons of Edinburgh* (ISBN-13: 978-0748615674) and *Physicians, Surgeons and Apothecaries: Medical Practice in Seventeenth-century Edinburgh* (ISBN-13: 978-1898410461)

In 1645, George Rae was offered £100 by the council to be the plague doctor, when his predecessor, John Paulitious died after a short time on the job. Rae continually asked the council for the money they'd promised, but it is doubtful they ever paid him. His wife and child died from the plague. McCrae isn't based on Rae, but the book was inspired by Rae's story.

Disenchanted

C L Raven

Once upon a time, in lands far, far away, everyone lived happily ever after. Until now. If you thought you knew the fairytales well, think again. In a modern world without morals, where beauty does not always equal goodness and evil sometimes wins, the heroes of the legends learn the hard way that survival will take more than just a pretty face, and a handsome prince does not mean salvation. Ten broken fairytales that are definitely not for children's bedtime.

Soul Asylum

C L Raven

The blood wanted to prick a conscience that couldn't bleed.
Poe could keep his telltale heart.
I couldn't hear it beating.

Ravens Retreat harbours a sinister secret. Inside its blackened heart lurk the ghosts of patients and staff who died when the asylum was burned down in 1904. Over a hundred years later, the West wing survives and now the patients want revenge.

Their eternal repose is disturbed by a malevolent poltergeist and the ghost tours led by the asylum's resident, Phineas Soul, which attract the attention of journalist Mason Strider. His attempts to expose Phineas as a fraud have catastrophic consequences when it is Ravens Retreat's dark heart that's exposed as it awakens to claim the lives of those who dare to enter its brutal past.

Some things should never be disturbed.

DEADLY REFLECTIONS

C L RAVEN

Death is only the beginning...

You're born, you live and you die. And sometimes, you come back.

When the veil between life and death is torn down, the darkest souls crawl from the shadows to wander the world that rejected them.

But these are not the restless spirits that haunt the pages of folklore, or the childishly gruesome tales whispered over torchlight. These are the ghosts that dwell in the deepest dungeons of your imagination and prey on you when you think you're alone: bored ghosts trapped in the monotony of office life at the Scare Department; a haunted jail where the prisoners believe in revenge over rehabilitation; a mirror that steals the souls of whoever falls under its spell; and a ghost bride who makes sure the wedding vows are never broken.

Thirteen stories that prove the monsters in your mind might just be real.

The past is no longer a nightmare.

ROMANCE IS DEAD

C L RAVEN

Don't give your lover roses, give them nightmares.

Ten disturbing stories about the dangers of falling in love. Nothing says 'I love you' like giving your lover a heart for Valentine's. Especially when it's ripped from their body before they've drawn their last breath.

"I'd made a terrible mistake. I should have killed him in the shower."

Gone are the expensive chocolates in fancy packaging, the wilting roses from the petrol station forecourt and the heart-print boxer shorts. Valentine's is about to get bloody. And some unfortunate lovers will learn the true meaning of 'til death us do part.'

Real love is worth killing for.

Made in the USA
Charleston, SC
23 April 2016